i WILL
ALWAYS
LOVE YOU

Published in 2019 by Hardie Grant Books,
an imprint of Hardie Grant Publishing

Hardie Grant Books (London)
5th & 6th Floors
52–54 Southwark Street
London, SE1 1UN

Hardie Grant Books (Melbourne)
Building 1, 658 Church Street
Richmond, Victoria 3121

hardiegrantbooks.com

Originally published by Editorial Planeta, S.A., 2018

British Library Cataloguing-in-Publication Data. A catalogue record for this book
is available from the British Library.

I Will Always Love You
ISBN: 9781784882761

Publishing Director: Kate Pollard
Junior Editor: Bex Fitzsimons
Translator: Gilla Evans
Editor: Kay Delves
Proofreader: Sarah Herman

Colour reproduction by p2d
Printed and bound in China by Leo Paper Products Ltd.

10 9 8 7 6 5 4 3 2 1

I WILL ALWAYS LOVE YOU

THE LOVES, BREAK-UPS AND SONGS THAT HAVE MADE HISTORY

Marisa Morea

CONTENTS

I

WiLL

~~ALWAYS~~

LOVE

YOU

I'm terrified of the word «always». It's a prison, a shackle chaining you to eternity. A passport that makes you a slave to your words if you're the kind of person who is consistent in what you say and what you do, in what you think and what you feel. This innocent-seeming adverb makes me feel morally obliged not to contradict myself and yet, when I'm thirsty I'd like to be able to drink this water without getting poisoned.

I repeat: I'm terrified of the word «always», even more so when it comes with an «I love you». I've never said, «I will always love you» and I haven't liked it on those occasions when it's been said to me. Out of this absurd phobia about eternity and my fascination for music comes this book.

« I Will Always Love You » takes you on a journey through the top love stories of the music world through great songs, and vice versa. Couples who were together both personally and professionally and who made us believe in eternal love. Grand passions that have left behind them only ashes and beautiful songs.

« I Will Always Love You » is an excuse to talk about love and other things, about records that gave me the shivers, about CBGB, about jazz, about when Leonard met Janis in a lift in the Chelsea Hotel, about Lola Flores, about drugs, about Obama or about « West Side Story ».

BECAUSE WE HAVE LEARNT
THAT
« living happily ever after »
IS SOMETHING THAT
HAPPENS ONLY TO
A FEW,
although the rest of us
will ALWAYS have our
FAVOURITE RECORDS,
the ones that make
OUR HEARTS
sing.

ETERNAL FLAME

(while it lasted)

PJ HARVEY & NICK CAVE (1996)

DORSET

<<TO BRING YOU MY LOVE>> (1995)

In 1995, after spending a year writing songs in a rural retreat in Somerset, PJ Harvey released her third studio album, *To Bring You My Love*. The record received rave reviews, was nominated for a Grammy and the Mercury Prize, and kept the musician on the road touring for nearly a year. This left her worn out physically and emotionally, so she went home to the countryside to recover the strength that would allow her to return three years later.

LEAD TRACK!
<<DOWN by the WATER>>
ABOUT A CRAZED MOTHER DROWNING HER DAUGHTER IN THE RIVER.

« MURDER BALLADS »
(1996)

Those who rate Nick Cave as a songwriter
would not have been surprised when
the Prince of Darkness released *Murder
Ballads* (1996), an album of macabre fables
that recreated crimes of all kinds and their
consequences. Nick recorded two duets
in *Murder Ballads*.

« Where the Wild
Roses Grow »

with KYLIE
MINOGUE

(the story of a man
who woos a woman
while planning
to take her life)

« Henry
Lee »

with PJ
HARVEY

(the story of a woman who is
rejected sexually by a married
man and then stabs him to death)

Nick and PJ got to know each other when making the video of 'Henry Lee', which captured them falling in love. It was recorded in a single take of almost four minutes, with them looking into each other's eyes, without any rehearsal or choreography. Their attraction was so magnetic that the video ends with their first kiss.

NICK WAS IN THE PROCESS OF DIVORCING HIS BRAZILIAN WIFE VIVIANE CARNEIRO, WITH WHOM HE HAD HAD HIS SON, LUKE, IN 1991, THE SAME YEAR THAT HIS SON JETHRO WAS BORN TO A DIFFERENT MOTHER IN AUSTRALIA.

The relationship between Nick and PJ was not confirmed by either of them until it ended, just a few months later.

THE ALBUM

« THE BOATMAN'S CALL » BY NICK CAVE & THE BAD SEEDS (1998)

INCLUDED THE SONGS

West Country Girl & *Black Hair*

INSPIRED BY NICK'S FEELINGS FOR PJ.

Following their break-up, the Australian took to using heroin more intensely. He had been addicted since his early days with the band The Birthday Party.

The Birthday Party,

PREVIOUSLY KNOWN AS THE BOYS NEXT DOOR, WAS AN AUSTRALIAN POST-PUNK BAND LED BY NICK CAVE. THEY MOVED FROM MELBOURNE TO LONDON AND THEN TO BERLIN, WHERE THEY SOON BECAME INVOLVED IN THE ARTISTIC VANGUARD, THRASHED BY DRUGS AND THEIR VIOLENT PUNCHES.

For her part, PJ considered giving up music and going off to be a nurse in Africa (as told in her biography *Siren Rising* by James R. Blandford). Luckily, she didn't, and instead she put together a new album:

« IS THIS DESIRE ? » (1998)

Although on a personal level they were too heavy and sombre when together, Nick and PJ did inspire one another, giving us some great songs. We must face up to our problems and responsibilities alone in the end.

SONNY & CHER
(1962-1979)

Cher and Sonny Bono met in a café in Los Angeles in 1962 when she was only sixteen – eleven years younger than him – and had just left school to pursue her dream of becoming a star. She had not had an easy life until then, travelling all over the country as her mother changed husbands, and she was used to all kinds of difficulties.

Sonny was working as a production assistant for music producer Phil Spector in Gold Star Studios.

Phil Spector

WAS THE CREATOR OF AN UNPRECEDENTED KIND OF MUSIC PRODUCTION,

THE WALL OF SOUND.

WITH IT HE CREATED A DENSE REVERB SOUND,

RECORDING LOTS OF LAYERS OF SOUND WITH ACOUSTIC

AND ELECTRIC GUITARS AND INSTRUMENTAL ARRANGEMENTS,

EQUIVALENT TO AN ORCHESTRA IN AN ECHO CHAMBER.

<< River Deep - Mountain High >>,
by
Ike and Tina Turner,

WAS THE HIGH POINT OF HIS WALL OF SOUND PRODUCTIONS.

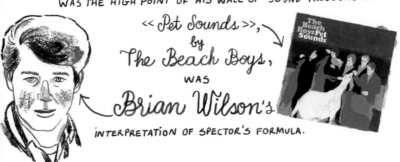

<< Pet Sounds >>,
by
The Beach Boys,
WAS
Brian Wilson's

INTERPRETATION OF SPECTOR'S FORMULA.

A short while after Sonny and Cher met, Cher's flatmate left the apartment they shared, and Cher accepted Sonny's offer to be his housekeeper. Their friendship grew, until they became a couple in 1964.

Through Bono, Cher began as a session singer doing backing vocals for Phil Spector's productions, such as 'Be My Baby', by The Ronettes.

Phil Spector WAS MARRIED FROM 1968 TO 1974 TO *Ronnie Spector*, OF *The* **Ronettes**, A NEW YORK GIRL GROUP THAT WAS ACTIVE UNTIL 1967. AS SOON AS RONNIE MARRIED PHIL, HE LOCKED HER UP IN HIS LOS ANGELES MANSION. THE SINGER'S MOTHER CAME TO HER RESCUE AND TOGETHER THEY PLANNED HER ESCAPE FROM THE HOUSE.

In 1965 Sonny and Cher began singing together songs written, arranged and produced by Sonny in the Spector style. To begin with they were called Caesar & Cleo, but for their first record, *Look at Us*, they changed to Sonny & Cher. They won huge acclaim with the single 'I Got You Babe', which went to number one.

Their second album, *The Wondrous World of Sonny & Cher* (1966), was a resounding success. They embarked on a world tour and appeared on prime-time TV shows.

The cherry on top of their success came with the single 'The Beat Goes On', included in their third album, *In Case You're in Love* (1967).

Cher

BECAME A STYLE ICON
IN THE SEVENTIES.

with her
big fringe

bellbottoms

and
ultra-black
eyeliner

her
extravagant
prints

When the seventies came to an end, the monogamous, drug-free life of Sonny & Cher was going out of fashion, as was their music, with the emergence of hard rock, psychedelia and bands such as Jefferson Airplane and Cream.

Their relationship began to get complicated too. Sonny's repeated infidelities were forgiven with the birth of their daughter, Chastity, and then again with their marriage in 1969.

Almost finished professionally and struggling for money, in 1970 the duo began to perform in nightclubs in Las Vegas. The delivery of their songs was so lacklustre and depressing that they were booed by the audience. Cher responded, Sonny tried to hush her and she told him to shut up. The matrimonial dispute on stage went down well as a kind of variety show, and they were hired for their own television show, *The Sonny & Cher Comedy Hour* (1971), which was broadcast for three years.

WERE SOME OF THE GUESTS THEY INTERVIEWED BETWEEN THEIR COMEDY SKETCHES, IN WHICH THEY SOMETIMES INCLUDED THEIR DAUGHTER CHASTITY, PUTTING ON A FAKE SEMBLANCE OF THE IDEAL FAMILY.

In the third season of *The Sonny & Cher Comedy Hour*, the couple were going through their worst times and ended up separating a few months later, in 1975.

Three days after their divorce, Cher married musician Greg Allman, founder of The Allman Brothers Band, but she filed for divorce nine days later because of her husband's heroin and alcohol problems. The couple were, however, reconciled. They had a child and released a very poor record under the pitiful name of *Allman and Woman*, and their relationship carried on until 1979.

DEBBIE HARRY & CHRIS STEIN
(1974 - 1989)

Debby Harry met Chris Stein when she was leading the band The Stilettos, struggling to survive as a singer in 1974 New York. In her second gig at The Boburn Tavern, Chris Stein was in the audience. At the end of the concert Debbie approached him. By the end of the night she had invited him to join The Stilettos as guitarist.

BORN IN MIAMI, Debbie WAS ADOPTED AT THE AGE OF THREE MONTHS AND BROUGHT UP IN New Jersey. HER PARENTS DIDN'T UNDERSTAND THE LIFE SHE LED IN THE BIG APPLE, WHERE SHE WORKED AS A WAITRESS, A GO-GO DANCER AND A Playboy BUNNY.

The chemistry between Debbie and Chris grew steadily, and after three months they began to go out together and to compose songs for the band. When The Stilettos dissolved, Debbie and Chris formed Blondie in October 1974.

THE NAME *Blondie* (THE GROUP STARTED OUT AS *Angel & The Snake*) CAME FROM THE CATCALL SO OFTEN DIRECTED AT DEBBIE.

Blondie regularly performed in clubs such as Max's Kansas City – a top haunt of glam rock and then punk – and CBGB. It was not long before they had signed a record contract, overtaking many of the groups in that scene. In 1976, they launched their debut album, *Blondie*, which was not a great commercial success.

CBGB

(ACRONYM OF *Country Bluegrass and Blues*) WAS OPENED BY *Hilly Kristal* IN 1973. ALTHOUGH INITIALLY SET UP TO HOST COUNTRY AND BLUES CONCERTS, TOWARDS THE END OF THE SEVENTIES IT BECAME THE EPICENTRE OF THE NEW YORK PUNK ROCK AND NEW WAVE SCENE, FEATURING GROUPS SUCH AS

The Ramones, Television, Patti Smith Group, Blondie and Talking Heads.

MUSICIANS HAD TO BRING THEIR OWN EQUIPMENT AND HAVE THEIR OWN ORIGINAL REPERTOIRE ; COVER BANDS WERE NOT WELCOME.

In 1977 Blondie released their second album, *Plastic Letters*, but it wasn't until *Parallel Lines* in 1978 that they achieved worldwide success. Debbie Harry immediately became an icon, a sort of punk Marilyn. All the girls wanted to be her and all the boys wanted to meet her. Platinum blonde hair and her trademark T-shirt became fashionable. The look of Madonna or Cindy Lauper would have been inconceivable without Debbie Harry, who, along with Patti Smith and Siouxie, changed the look of women in the music world.

<< Heart Of Glass >>

COMPOSED JOINTLY BY Chris and Debbie, WAS HIGHLY CONTROVERSIAL FOR ITS MUSICAL ARRANGEMENTS. THE MOST PURIST OF THE NEW WAVE ACCUSED THEM OF SELLING OUT WITH A COMMERCIAL SOUND THAT THE UNDERGROUND SCENE UTTERLY REJECTED. FROM THEN ON, Blondie BECAME THE TOP POP BAND.

With their success things around them changed. Debbie's styling was now in the hands of Stephen Sprouse, and the singer began to frequent new circles, such as Studio 54, where she met her friend Andy Warhol. But the relationship between Chris and Debbie was solid as a rock. In spite of Debbie's open bisexuality and her heroin addition, they stayed together for several more years.

The worst was still to come. During the promotional tour of their sixth album, Chris collapsed after a show and was hospitalised. He was seriously ill with *pemphigus vulgaris*, an autoimmune disease of the skin. It took him four years to recover.

POISON IVY and LUX INTERIOR, OF THE CRAMPS WERE ONE OF THE MOST CREATIVE COUPLES OF PUNK ROCK. PSYCHOBILLY BEGAN WITH THEIR PUNK REINTERPRETATION OF FIFTIES ROCKABILLY. AFTER THIRTY-SEVEN YEARS TOGETHER, LUX DIED IN 2007.

Chris's illness, their drug abuse and various problems of financial management and poor ticket sales for their concerts led to the break-up of Blondie at the end of 1982.

From then on, Debbie concentrated on her solo records and her acting career. In 1988 she appeared in *Hairspray*, by John Waters, with whom she had collaborated along with Chris composing the soundtrack of the short film *Polyester* in 1981.

Chris and Debbie stayed together for a while longer until Chris recovered. They finally split in 1989 after sixteen years together.

Blondie
REUNITED IN 1997. IN 1999 *Chris* MARRIED AGAIN AND HAD TWO DAUGHTERS. *Debbie* HAS NO CHILDREN, NOR HAS SHE HAD ANY LASTING RELATIONSHIPS AFTER ENDING THINGS WITH CHRIS.

JANE BIRKIN & SERGE GAINSBOURG

(1968 - 1982)

Jane Birkin happened to meet Serge Gainsbourg when auditioning for the film *Slogan* by Pierre Grimblat, and she thought him a vile old narcissist. Jane had just been abandoned by her husband, John Barry, composer of the soundtrack for the *James Bond* series and later for the moving *Out of Africa* theme. One day, Barry went off to Los Angeles without leaving so much as a note. Aged just twenty-one and recently having given birth to their daughter, Birkin flew from London to Paris to take the audition in spite of hardly being able to speak a word of French. She was in such a state that, on seeing her burst into tears in one of the scenes, the director decided that Serge and Jane should star in his film.

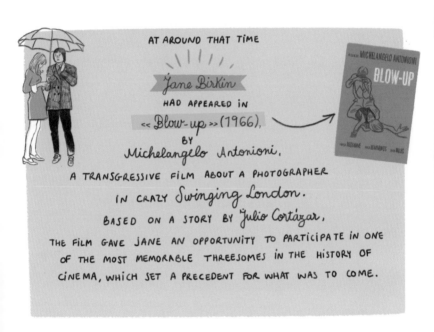

AT AROUND THAT TIME

Jane Birkin

HAD APPEARED IN

« Blow-up » (1966),

BY

Michelangelo Antonioni.

A TRANSGRESSIVE FILM ABOUT A PHOTOGRAPHER IN CRAZY Swinging London. BASED ON A STORY BY Julio Cortázar, THE FILM GAVE JANE AN OPPORTUNITY TO PARTICIPATE IN ONE OF THE MOST MEMORABLE THREESOMES IN THE HISTORY OF CINEMA, WHICH SET A PRECEDENT FOR WHAT WAS TO COME.

That Serge had a way with women was already obvious from the intense romance he had had with Brigitte Bardot, who in 1967 was married to playboy Gunter Sachs. Serge, who was crazy about her, wrote 'Initials B.B.' and together they recorded *Serge Gainsbourg and Brigitte Bardot: Bonnie and Clyde* (1968). She later inspired the sensual 'Je t'aime ... moi non plus', a sexually explicit song in which Brigitte's moans are an ode to the female orgasm.

IN THE END
THE RECORDING MADE WITH
Brigitte Bardot
WAS NOT RELEASED. HER HUSBAND GOT WIND OF IT AND
THREATENED HER WITH HIS LAWYERS LEFT, RIGHT AND
CENTRE. FEARING REPRISALS, BRIGITTE ASKED SERGE NOT TO
RELEASE IT, AND SHE WENT BACK TO HER HUSBAND
AS A GOOD, REPENTANT WIFE.

The end of the affair.

At the end of that year Serge decided to move on when he met Jane Birkin and together they recorded 'Je t'aime ... moi non plus' again. Jane recorded it an octave higher than Bardot, which added to her 'Lolita' image. The single was released in February 1969. It was a success and a scandal; it was banned by the Vatican and restricted to those over twenty-one in France.

Brigitte Bardot

CONSENTED TO HER VERSION BEING RELEASED IN 1986
IN EXCHANGE FOR ANY PROFITS BEING PASSED ON TO
HER ANIMAL CHARITY.

The over-ten-year relationship between Jane and Serge was something of a roller-coaster. Drinking to excess, high-profile rows, night-time outings and passionate reconciliations were an explosive mix. In 1971, their daughter, Charlotte, was born, and the same year Serge released *Histoire de Melody Nelson*, a twenty-eight-minute concept album with a *Lolita*-esque narrative. It is my favourite of his records, featuring Jane Birkin on the cover and on vocals, with choral arrangements by Jean-Claude Vannier, which make this album a masterpiece.

THE FIRST TO EMBODY THE MYTH OF LOLITA
IN THE SPANISH MUSIC WORLD WAS
Lola Flores

TOGETHER WITH HER ARTISTIC AND ROMANTIC PARTNER
Manolo Caracol.

THE GAP BETWEEN THEM WAS ONLY FOURTEEN YEARS
BUT SEEMED MORE. THEY MADE THEIR DEBUT IN 1943
WITH THEIR MUSICAL SHOW
« *Zambra* »
AND IN 1951 THEY WENT THEIR SEPARATE WAYS.

Charlotte was always with them, even when they went out at night, when she was still young enough to be put in the iconic wicker basket that Jane always carried. When Charlotte grew older, Jane would get up when the girl came home from school and spend the afternoon with her. Once Charlotte had gone to bed, Serge and Jane would go off to a nightclub. When they got home, Charlotte would get up and go to school and they would go to sleep.

Charlotte Gainsbourg IS TODAY ONE OF EUROPE'S MOST HIGHLY REGARDED ACTRESSES, A MUSE FOR Lars von Trier AND WINNER OF THE AWARD FOR Best Actress at Cannes FOR << Antichrist >> IN 2009, WHEN SHE ALSO RELEASED HER THIRD STUDIO ALBUM, << IRM >>, PRODUCED BY Beck.

Roger Vadim's erotic feature-length film *If Don Juan Were a Woman* starred Brigitte Bardot as the mythical Don Juan narrating all her amorous adventures in flashback. One of these adventures was with a much younger woman, and the role was offered to Jane Birkin, who accepted without any qualms. A still in which the naked beauty of Birkin and Bardot is seen was considered nirvana.

A short time afterwards Jane decided to leave Serge. Gainsbourg's alcoholism had turned him violent and Jane wanted to end the relationship. Besides, she was beginning to be attracted to other men, such as French film director Jacques Doillon, with whom she went on to have another daughter, Lou, in 1982, not long after her split from Serge.

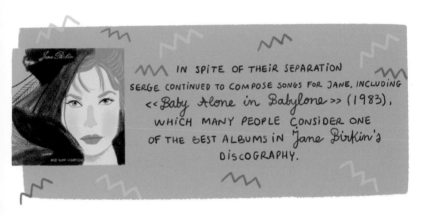

IN SPITE OF THEIR SEPARATION SERGE CONTINUED TO COMPOSE SONGS FOR JANE, INCLUDING << Baby Alone in Babylone >> (1983), WHICH MANY PEOPLE CONSIDER ONE OF THE BEST ALBUMS IN Jane Birkin's DISCOGRAPHY.

Jane and Serge remained friends and collaborated professionally until Gainsbourg's death from a heart attack in 1991. Deeply saddened, Jane, who lost her father two days later, spent three days shut away with Serge's body. In his coffin, Serge was laid to rest with Jane's childhood toy, Monkey, the one that had appeared on the cover of *Histoire de Melody Nelson*. Just three days before he died he had given her a precious diamond. Jane knew that Serge had died still in love with her and composing for her. Incapable of competing with the love story between Serge and Jane, Jacques Doillon, now something of a legend in French popular culture, left Jane.

JUNE CARTER & JOHNNY CASH
(1956-2003)

Johnny Cash and June Carter met in the mid-fifties behind the scenes at the Grand Ole Opry theatre in Nashville. June, who was part of the country music dynasty The Carter Family, was performing with her sisters in The Carter Sisters and doing vocals for Elvis. By chance, Johnny Cash was performing his debut that night. They soon fell in love, although June didn't give in so readily.

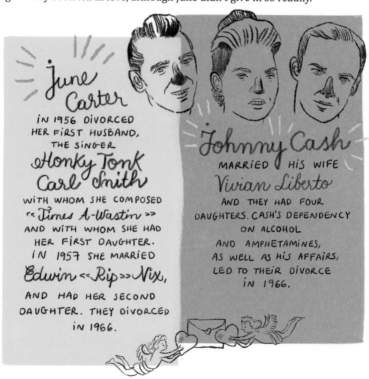

June Carter
IN 1956 DIVORCED HER FIRST HUSBAND, THE SINGER *Honky Tonk Carl Smith* WITH WHOM SHE COMPOSED << *Time's A-Wastin* >> AND WITH WHOM SHE HAD HER FIRST DAUGHTER. IN 1957 SHE MARRIED *Edwin << Rip >> Nix*, AND HAD HER SECOND DAUGHTER. THEY DIVORCED IN 1966.

Johnny Cash
MARRIED HIS WIFE *Vivian Liberto* AND THEY HAD FOUR DAUGHTERS. CASH'S DEPENDENCY ON ALCOHOL AND AMPHETAMINES, AS WELL AS HIS AFFAIRS, LED TO THEIR DIVORCE IN 1966.

After flirting with the idea of becoming an actress, June returned to music in earnest when The Carters joined Johnny's tour. He had been crazy about her ever since they met. It was 1961.

In 1963 June Carter wrote 'Ring of Fire' with Merle Kilgore, which Johnny Cash recorded. It went to number one and was the biggest success of his career.

« Ring of Fire »

RELATES THE INEVITABLE PASSION THAT BROUGHT

June & Johnny

TOGETHER IN SPITE OF THEIR BEING
MARRIED TO OTHER PEOPLE.

Collaborations between them were becoming increasingly frequent. Johnny and June recorded 'It Ain't Me Babe' by Bob Dylan for Johnny Cash's album *Orange Blossom Special* (1965), which was a great success. In 1967 they performed the song 'Jackson' together, which won them a Grammy for the Best Country & Western Performance by a Duo, Trio or Group.

Johnny brought the secrecy of their romance to an end when he asked June Carter to marry him in front of a crowd of seven thousand when performing at the London Ice House in Ontario. They married in Franklin, Kentucky, on 1 March 1968. Their only child was born two years later.

THEIR SON ARRIVED IN 1970 ALONG WITH THEIR SECOND GRAMMY FOR THEIR VERSION OF

<< *If I were a Carpenter* >>
BY Tim Hardin

During the seventies they continued working, touring and struggling with Johnny's addictions and his self-destructive nature. Carter remained at her partner's side for thirty-five years of checking in and out of rehab centres and relapses, until she died in 2003. Johnny Cash followed her to a better place four months later.

Johnny Cash
WAS INDUCTED INTO THE
Rock & Roll Hall of Fame
IN 1992, BUT HIS DIVERSITY ALSO PUT HIM INTO THE

Nashville Songwriters Hall of Fame (1977)

Country Music Hall of Fame (1980)

Gospel Music Hall of Fame (2010)

Memphis Music Hall of Fame (2013)

MARIANNE FAITHFULL & MICK JAGGER
(1966-1970)

Back in 1964 Marianne Faithfull banged her fist on the table and announced that she would live her life her own way. The immaculate teenager from London high society wanted to be part of Swinging London. After the austerity period of the fifties following the Second World War, London was beginning to recover its zest for life and celebration, and young people carried the banner of the sixties with a revolutionary and transgressive hedonism. The Beatles, The Who, the miniskirt, *Blow-Up*, Richard Hamilton, mods ... and, of course, The Rolling Stones.

Mick Jagger and Keith Richards, two middle-class lads from the London suburbs, had already made a name for themselves with The Rolling Stones. In early 1964, at a party, the band's manager, Andrew Loog Oldham, took a fancy to a very young Marianne, saying, 'I'm going to make you a star.'

HER FIRST SUCCESS WAS
« As Tears Go By »,
ONE OF THE FIRST
COMPOSITIONS BY
Jagger & Keith,
WHO UNTIL THEN ONLY DID
STANDARD BLUES COVERS
WITH
The Rolling Stones.

Marianne won the hearts of the audience with her look of innocence, and also the heart of gallery owner John Dunbar, whom she married in 1965. She had her son, Nicholas Dunbar, at the age of only eighteen. She went on to have affairs with both Brian Jones and Keith Richards; and eventually left both her son and husband to go and live with Mick Jagger.

Jagger and Faithfull were the couple of the moment. Tired of hotels and theatres, they gave up touring to form the intimate circle of the Stones. Rock and roll, orgies and LSD: they were living it up.

Marianne

SAID IN AN INTERVIEW THAT WHEN HER SON, NOW AN ADULT, ASKED HER WHAT THE SIXTIES WERE LIKE, SHE SAID << Purple Haze >>, by Jimi Henderiss.

Keith Richards would invite friends and acquaintances to Redlands, his home on the south coast of England. People came and went according to their highs and their comedowns. It was there that, in February 1967, one of the biggest scandals of the acid era almost finished off The Rolling Stones. After a tip-off from their dealer, Jagger, Richards and the last guests to leave were caught by the police in possession of, and using, LSD, in the company of one mysterious woman, 'Miss X', as she was called by those who published the photos of Marianne naked, all skin and bones, half covered with a small rabbit-skin rug. This was a hammer blow for the virginal Marianne, who was unfairly mistreated as a woman and mother by the public, who, on the other hand, demanded the release of Keith Richards and Mick Jagger after a very high-profile trial in which they were sentenced to prison for drug possession and finally released on probation.

In 1979 Mick and Marianne broke up after a very intense four-year relationship, which included a miscarriage at seven months, numerous infidelities, addictions, the death of Brian Jones, who drowned in a swimming pool, and a suicide attempt that left Marianne in a coma for almost a week.

<< *Beggars Banquet* >>
(1968)

<< *Let It Bleed* >>
(1969)

<< *Sticky Fingers* >>
(1971)

But, they nevertheless left us a handful of legendary songs:

'Sympathy for the Devil' (1968), *Beggars Banquet*. Inspired by *The Master and Margarita* by Mikhail Bulgakov, a book given to Jagger by Faithfull.

'You Can't Always Get What You Want' (1969), *Let it Bleed*. Written and composed about Marianne and the party about to end that was the sixties.

'Wild Horses' (1971), *Sticky Fingers*. Although it was initially conceived by Richards as a lullaby for his son, Jagger rewrote it, recounting the end of his relationship with Marianne.

'Sister Morphine' (1971), *Sticky Fingers*. Co-written by Jagger, Richards and Faithfull, previously issued as a B-side in 1969.

A year after their split, Mick announced his marriage to Bianca Jagger. Marianne sank into a deep depression and became more self-destructive. Her addiction and her broken heart led to her losing everything: contact with her family, her friends, her musical career, her home and, worst of all, custody of her son. The ingénue of the early sixties ended the decade as a hippie, and in the early seventies ended up wandering the streets of London's Soho as a heroin addict for years.

Surprisingly, she survived.

<< Broken English >> (1979)
Marianne Faithfull

FOUND HER WAY BACK WITH THIS ALBUM, IN WHICH SHE DISPLAYS A NEW, DEEPER AND MORE GRAINY VOCAL PITCH, RESULTING FROM HER ADDICTIONS.

Since the mid-eighties, she has distanced herself from drugs and is now part of the generation that made history and is venerated by rock and roll. Mick and Marianne are no longer in contact with one another. You can forgive, but you don't forget.

HER ALBUM
<< Easy Come, Easy Go >>
IS A COLLECTION OF COVERS IN WHICH
SHE IS ACCOMPANIED BY
Rufus Wainwright, Jarvis Cocker,
Sean Lennon, Nick Cave
and Keith Richards.

BRETT ANDERSON & JUSTINE FRISCHMANN & DAMON ALBARN
(1989 - 1991) (1992-2000)

Brett Anderson and Justine Frischmann met at University College London in 1989 and soon started going out. Together with a childhood friend of Brett's, Matt Osman, they decided to form a group, but they needed a guitarist, so they placed an advert for one in the *NME*:

Young guitarist needed by London-based band. Smiths, Commotions, Bowie, Pet Shop Boys.
No Musos.
Some things are more important than ability.
Call Brett.

Among the responses was one from Bernard Butler, who ended up joining the band. As they had no drummer, they used a drum machine. They soon began to do small gigs around Camden. Suede was born.

Damon Albarn and Graham Coxon were childhood friends and they met Alex James when studying at Goldsmiths College. Damon had a band, Circus, in which Coxon and James ended up playing, renaming the band Seymour.

They played their first gig in the summer of 1989, and were signed up in the autumn by Food Records, a subsidiary of EMI, on the condition that they changed their name. And so, Blur was born.

Blur RELEASED THEIR FIRST ALBUM << *Leisure* >>, IN 1991.

Justine and Brett broke up in 1991. Frischmann had fallen in love with Blur's lead singer, despite still living with Brett. Although Justine thought that Brett and the group could contain the situation, the news came as a total shock and Justine ended up leaving and forming Elastica.

Britpop

Elastica

WAS BORN IN 1992 AND A YEAR LATER THEY RELEASED THEIR FIRST SINGLE, << *Stutter* >>. THEIR FIRST LP, << *Elastica* >>, WAS RELEASED IN 1995 AND BECAME THE FASTEST SELLING DEBUT ALBUM SINCE << *Definitely Maybe* >>, BY *Oasis*.

Suede recorded several demos with a new drummer and signed with the independent Nude Records to release a couple of singles. Just through word-of-mouth, Suede became very popular and music critics soon declared them the 'Best New Band in Britain'.

THEIR FIRST ALBUM, << *Suede* >>, RELEASED IN 1993, SHOWED A GREAT DEAL OF GLAM-ROCK AND PUNK INFLUENCE.

The love affair between Damon and Justine lasted eight years. The fame secured with their respective bands kept their relationship on the front pages, making them one of Britpop's most famous couples. This pressure, alongside being so young, Elastica's success in the States, and alcohol and heroin, all proved too much for them.

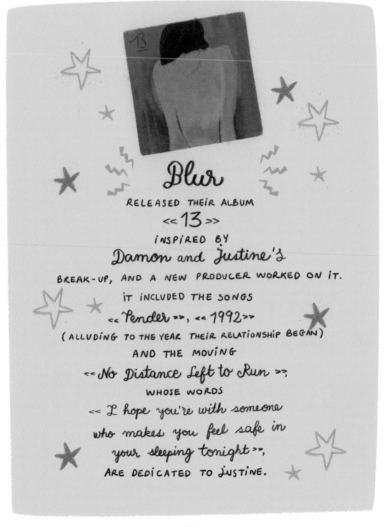

Blur
RELEASED THEIR ALBUM
<< 13 >>
INSPIRED BY
Damon and *Justine's*
BREAK-UP, AND A NEW PRODUCER WORKED ON IT.
IT INCLUDED THE SONGS
<< *Tender* >>, << *1992* >>
(ALLUDING TO THE YEAR THEIR RELATIONSHIP BEGAN)
AND THE MOVING
<< *No Distance Left to Run* >>,
WHOSE WORDS
<< *I hope you're with someone who makes you feel safe in your sleeping tonight* >>,
ARE DEDICATED TO *Justine*.

MILES DAVIS & JULIETTE GRÉCO
(1949–1951)

Paris
Saint-Germain-des-Prés

At the end of the forties, European society was marked by the injustice of the Second World War. Artists and philosophers filled the cabarets and cafés of Paris with smoke and poetry. A slim girl with big, dark eyes, dressed in black, was reciting poems by Queneau and Prévert in Le Tabou. It was Juliette Gréco, the muse of existentialism.

Le Tabou

WAS A JAZZ CLUB OPENED IN 1947 AT 33 RUE DAUPHINE. IT WAS THE FIRST EXISTENTIALIST CABARET AND MEETING PLACE FOR *Zazous,* YOUNG PEOPLE WHO WORE OVERSIZED ENGLISH OR AMERICAN CLOTHES AND WERE INTO BEBOP.

In these cafés, Juliette made friends with the likes of Boris Vian, Jean-Paul Sartre and Albert Camus. Because of their encouragement, and the poems they gave her to set to music, she began her singing career.

DURING THE SECOND WORLD WAR, *Paris* HAD BEEN OCCUPIED BY THE NAZIS. *Juliette,* HER SISTER AND HER MOTHER, WHO BELONGED TO THE RESISTANCE, WERE ARRESTED BY THE GESTAPO AND SENT TO A PRISON CAMP. AT THE AGE OF JUST SIXTEEN, JULIETTE WAS RELEASED AND FOUND HERSELF ALONE AND PENNILESS IN PARIS. SHE SOUGHT REFUGE IN THE HOME OF HER FRENCH TEACHER, WHERE SHE BEGAN TO DEVELOP AN INTEREST IN LITERATURE, ART AND THE COMMUNIST YOUTH MOVEMENT.

Meanwhile in New York, Miles Davis and Charlie Parker were the major exponents of bebop and spent most of the forties playing together. In 1948 Miles left Charlie and formed a band of nine musicians with an unusual wind section that went by The Miles Davis Nonet. They landed a contract with Capitol Records, and recorded twelve pieces for a record that was not very successful, but was a forerunner in the creation of cool jazz.

Capitol Records
RE-RELEASED THIS RECORD IN 1957 AS
<< *The Birth of Cool* >>.
THE
cool, or West Coast Jazz →
IS CHRONOLOGICALLY LATER THAN *bebop*
AND CONTEMPORARY WITH *hardbop*.

COOL JAZZ MOVED AWAY FROM THE FURIOUS
RHYTHMS OF BEPOP AND BECAME CALMER AND MORE
ELEGANT. COOL WAS THE JAZZ OF WHITE MUSICIANS, SUCH AS
Chet Baker, Stan Getz and *Gerry Mulligan*.
THE REJECTION OF JAZZ'S BLACK ORIGINS LED
MILES DAVIS TO LATER REPUDIATE COOL, IN SPITE
OF HAVING HAD A BIG INFLUENCE
ON ITS CREATION.

BIRTH OF THE COOL
miles davis

In 1949 Miles Davis travelled to Europe with a new group to perform at the Paris International Jazz Festival. Davis fell in love with the city and its existentialist bohemia, which adored bebop jazz. Furthermore, African-Americans were treated with greater respect there than in the United States, where racial segregation was rife.

Juliette Gréco met Miles Davis at the Salle Pleyel during one of his first concerts in Paris. All the tickets were sold and she would not have been able to afford one anyway, but Michelle Vian, Boris' wife, slipped her into the wings. Afterwards they all went to dine together. She spoke no English, he spoke no French, but the spark was ignited and they fell for one another.

The romance lasted long enough for Jean-Paul Sartre to ask Miles why they didn't get married. 'I love her too much to make her unhappy,' he replied. It was not a matter of disloyalty or betrayal, but of colour. Miles knew that if he took her to the racist America of the fifties with him, it would have destroyed her. The United States was not ready for a couple like them. Their affair ended officially, but they remained in touch in subsequent years.

HOWEVER, THE UNITED STATES WAS ANOTHER STORY IN THE NINETIES. *Lenny Kravitz* AND FRENCH SINGER *Vanessa Paradis* BEGAN THEIR ROMANCE IN 1992. THEY TRAVELLED TOGETHER TO AMERICA AND HE CO-WROTE AND PRODUCED THE SINGER'S FIRST RECORD IN ENGLISH. TOGETHER THEY PRODUCED SEVERAL DUETS, SUCH AS << *Silver and Gold* >> AND << *Lonely Rainbows* >>. THEIR RELATIONSHIP ENDED IN 1997.

Miles didn't hear Juliette sing until many years later, in 1957, when she travelled to New York to perform at the Waldorf Astoria. Afterwards they went to eat together and the waiter threw the food in their face because they were an interracial couple. It was very painful for Miles, who called Juliette in the early hours of the morning, crying and asking her not to see him again. It was confirmed: what they had was impossible.

THE LAST TIME THEY SAW ONE ANOTHER WAS A FEW MONTHS BEFORE MILES DIED, IN 1991, WHEN HE WENT TO VISIT HER IN HER PARIS HOME.

KIM GORDON & THURSTON MOORE
(1981-2011)

Thurston and Kim met in the East Village in the context of 'no wave', which promoted the experimental nature of music and rejected new wave as commercial. That year, Thurston and Kim formed Sonic Youth, pioneers of noise-rock and a later influence of nineties grunge.

DNA

Glenn Branca

Lydia Lunch

Teenage Jesus & the Jerks

84 ELDRIDGE ST.
NEW YORK 10002

IN SEPTEMBER 1988, IN THEIR NEW YORK APARTMENT,
THURSTON AND KIM RECORDED A SMALL HOME DOCUMENTARY,
WHICH CAN BE SEEN ON YOUTUBE.

Kim had moved to a small apartment on Eldridge Street, and one night she invited Thurston in. All she had was a foam mattress and a battered old guitar, which the previous tenant had left behind. Thurston recognised this guitar. It had belonged to his bandmate in The Coachmen, his recently disbanded group. He sat down and began to play it. That was their first night together.

Sonic Youth

CAME INTO MY WORLD AS A TEENAGER, BUT IT WASN'T UNTIL A FEW YEARS LATER THAT i WAS READY TO LOVE THEM. I HAD TO PASS THROUGH

<< *Rather Ripped* >>

BEFORE BEING ABLE TO ENJOY

<< *Sister* >>.

NOW THEIR DISCOGRAPHY IS IN MY TOP 10.

«SONIC NURSE»
(GEFFEN RECORDS, 2004)
TOP HIT!
«Dude Ranch Nurse»

THE COVER BELONGS TO THE
NURSE PAINTINGS SERIES BY RICHARD PRINCE.

Kim and Thurston married in 1984. It was not until 1994 that their daughter, Coco, was born. Over the years they showed us that family routine can be compatible with the turbulent life of a noise-rock band, constantly surrounded by the great icons of music in their social life.

CHLOË SEVIGNY

APPEARS IN THE SONIC YOUTH VIDEO CLIP
« *Sugar Kane* » (1993)
IN WHICH THE BAND PLAYS IN THE MIDDLE OF A FASHION SHOW BY A VERY YOUNG *Marc Jacobs*.

COURTNEY LOVE

IN 1991 HOLE RELEASED ITS DEBUT ALBUM
« *Pretty on the Inside* »
PRODUCED BY KIM GORDON.

KURT COBAIN

MONTHS BEFORE THEIR SMASH HIT
WITH
« *Nevermind* »
NIRVANA WENT ON A TOUR OF EUROPE WITH SONIC YOUTH. THERE THEY RECORDED THE DOCUMENTARY
« 1991 - THE YEAR PUNK BROKE ».

After sixteen studio albums, seven EPs, forty-six music videos and various contributions to soundtracks and other compilations, it's hard to believe that such an unconventional band should fall apart for a reason so common and hackneyed.

In 2005, publisher Eva Prinz commissioned Thurston to write and co-publish *Mix Tape: The Art of Cassette Culture*. Out of this project they created the publishing house Ecstatic Peace Library. The intimacy between them grew and, after a while, Thurston found himself embroiled in an emotional double life.

Sonic Youth moved to the stylish independent label Matador, and Mark Ibold, of Pavement, joined the group as its new bassist so that Kim could explore the electric guitar more. While Sonic Youth was renewing itself with the launch of its new record, their marriage was in its death throes.

Recording 'Anti-Orgasm' cannot have been easy, with the sensual phrasing of coming and going between Thurston and Kim, when she had known of her husband's affair with Eva for several months. No therapy, no redemptions, no ultimatums – nothing can keep someone at your side who has decided to move on.

<<MASSAGE THE HISTORY>>
IS THE ONLY SONG ON
<<The Eternal>>
THAT TALKS ABOUT THE END OF THEIR
MARRIAGE. IN IT, KIM ASKS THURSTON
TO COME BACK TO HER.

In 2011 Thurston Moore released his third solo album, *Demolished Thoughts*. An album of great sensitivity inspired by obsessive love, in which all the lyrics 'are a collection of sophomoric, self-obsessed, mostly acoustic mini suicide notes,' about Eva Prinz, as we can read in Gordon's memoir.

Eva

Two years of false promises later, Kim felt obliged to end their relationship after discovering a trail of clues that revealed her husband's successive infidelities with the same woman. I imagine that Thurston was aware that his divorce would mean the death of Sonic Youth and that, ultimately, leaving his family meant splitting from the band.

THE FINAL PERFORMANCE OF SONIC YOUTH
WAS AT THE SWU MUSIC & ARTS
FESTIVAL OF SÃO PAULO IN 2011.

BOB DYLAN & JOAN BAEZ
(1961-1965)

When, at the age of twenty, Bob Dylan arrived in New York from Minnesota, Joan Baez had already been crowned Queen of Folk. Joan, of Mexican-Scottish descent, performed her debut in 1959 at the Newport Folk Festival and released her first record, *Joan Baez*, in 1960, singing versions of traditional folk songs.

The
Newport Folk Festival
IS A MUSICAL EVENT FOUNDED BY
George Wein
IN NEWPORT, RHODE ISLAND. IT WAS FIRST HELD IN JULY 1959, PROMOTING POPULAR MUSIC AS A TOOL FOR ORDINARY PEOPLE TO CHAMPION THEIR RIGHTS AND FIGHT TO CREATE A MORE EGALITARIAN SOCIETY.

FOLK, BLUES, COUNTRY AND BLUEGRASS MUSICIANS, SUCH AS
Muddy Waters, Leonard Cohen, Bob Dylan, Joan Baez, Janis Joplin, Joni Mitchell
and
Miss Mama Thornton,
WERE ON THE BILL UNTIL 1970, ITS LAST EVENT UNTIL 1990 WHEN THE FESTIVAL WAS REVIVED!

Joan Baez soon realised that her concerts were a space for black and white people to meet, and she became an activist for civil rights. She always used her influence for social causes, such as racial integration or the protest against the Vietnam War.

In November 1961, Baez played a sell-out performance at The Town Hall, in what was her first major New York concert.

HER SECOND ALBUM,

Joan Baez in concert, Vol. 2 (1961),

WAS A GOLD DISC, AS WERE THE FOLLOWING TWO,

Joan Baez in concert, Part 1 (1962), and

Joan Baez in concert, Part 2 (1963),

IN WHICH HER FIRST INTERPRETATIONS OF DYLAN SONGS APPEAR,

« *With God on Our Side* » and

« *Don't Think Twice, It's All Right* ».

Joan was impressed when she first saw Bob Dylan perform one night in 1961 at Gerde's Folk City.

Gerde's FOLK CITY

WAS A NIGHTCLUB IN
Greenwich Village
WHERE LOTS OF SINGER-SONGWRITERS
OF THE SIXTIES AND SEVENTIES,
SUCH AS
The Mamas and the Papas,
Jimi Hendrix
and The Youngbloods, PERFORMED.

Bob Dylan
PERFORMED THERE PROFESSIONALLY FOR THE FIRST
TIME IN APRIL 1961 AS A WARM-UP FOR
John Lee Hooker.

AFTER THE PUBLICATION OF A FABULOUS REVIEW IN
<<THE NEW YORK TIMES>> IN SEPTEMBER, DYLAN MADE
A NAME FOR HIMSELF ON THE SCENE.

But they did not meet again until 1963, at Club 47 in Boston. A few weeks after that meeting, Joan Baez went up on stage at the Monterey Folk Festival to sing 'With God on Our Side' with Dylan. It was to be the start of a love story and of a series of legendary collaborations in the history of folk music.

In July 1963 Bob Dylan performed at the Newport Folk Festival for the first time. At the end, Joan invited Dylan to join her on her summer tour. Joan made Dylan the focus of attention, introducing him to audiences of ten thousand people. The Queen of Folk played a pivotal role in Bob Dylan's road to success, and his career was established after the release of his second album *The Freewheelin' Bob Dylan*.

This album was the first to contain his own compositions, alongside versions of classic blues and rock covers. Its first track, 'Blowin' in the Wind', which reflected in rhetorical questions on peace, war and freedom, would become a pacifist anthem in the sixties. Apart from socio-political themes, the album included romantic ballads and songs written in a humorous vein, showing his versatility as a songwriter.

THE COVER OF
The Freewheelin' Bob Dylan
IS A PORTRAIT TAKEN
BY PHOTOGRAPHER
Don Hunstein
OF THE MUSICIAN AND HIS GIRLFRIEND
AT THE TIME,
Suze Rotolo,
WALKING ALONG JONES STREET AND WEST
4TH STREET NEAR THE APARTMENT WHERE
THE COUPLE LIVED. DYLAN AND SUZE MET IN
1961 AND SPLIT UP WHEN HE BEGAN HIS
RELATIONSHIP WITH JOAN BAEZ.

Bob Dylan had become the voice of a generation. However, he changed course in 1965 with his fifth album, *Bringing It All Back Home*, with its electric A-side and acoustic B-side. Increasingly less interested in social problems and more focused on poetry that asked philosophical and religious questions, he moved away from his acoustic folk guitar and took up a Fender Stratocaster and began to sport a leather jacket.

What had seemed to be an eccentricity became his new signature when he released *Highway 61 Revisited* and his single 'Like a Rolling Stone', with a totally rock sound. This is how he presented himself at the Newport Folk Festival in 1965 and all hell broke loose.

He went up on stage with his black leather jacket, his Stratocaster and a full rock band: guitar, bass, organ and drums. They opened with a speeded-up version of 'Maggie's Farm' and the folk-song purists began to boo him above the rain of decibels. They followed with 'Like a Rolling Stone' and 'Phantom Engineer', but left the stage as soon as these were over.

The event's presenter asked Dylan to come back and play something else and he agreed, doing an acoustic mini-set of two hits: 'Mr Tambourine Man' and 'It's All Over Now, Baby Blue'. A last concession to those who wanted to see a performance from the folk singer-songwriter, who disappeared forever that night.

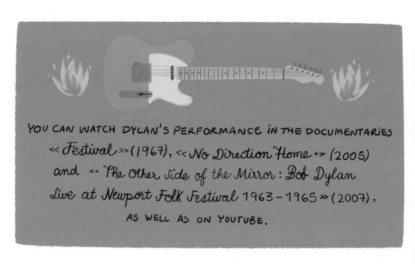

YOU CAN WATCH DYLAN'S PERFORMANCE IN THE DOCUMENTARIES
«Festival» (1967), «No Direction Home» (2005) and «The Other Side of the Mirror : Bob Dylan Live at Newport Folk Festival 1963 – 1965» (2007),
AS WELL AS ON YOUTUBE.

Later on, during his European tour, Bob Dylan invited Joan Baez to come and join him on stage. By then Dylan's career had eclipsed that of Baez, who was not going through the best of times, and this invitation was an attempt to reciprocate the help Joan had given him in his early years. But although she travelled to Europe, he didn't keep his word and, broken-hearted, Joan ended their two-year romance.

Bob Dylan MARRIED MODEL AND PLAYMATE *Sara Lownds,* WITH WHOM HE HAD FOUR CHILDREN, AMONG THEM *Jakob Dylan,* WHO IS ALSO A MUSICIAN AND IN THE NINETIES LED THE BAND *The Wallflowers.* THEY DIVORCED IN 1977.

In spite of Dylan's snub, in 1968 Joan Baez released *Any Day Now: Songs of Bob Dylan*. The same year she married pacifist leader David Harris, with whom she had a child before divorcing him in 1973. In 1972, she dedicated to her ex the song 'To Bobby', a wake-up call for him to return to social conscience and get involved in humanity's problems. Three years later Baez released *Diamonds and Rust*, one of her best records, whose eponymous song was written after Dylan called her to ask about her life. It seems that they mended fences, because that year they performed together again during Dylan's tour, Rolling Thunder Revue.

<< *Diamonds and Rust* >> WAS ADAPTED BY *Judas Priest* FOR THE RECORD << *Sin After Sin* >> IN 1977.

For their fans, Dylan and Baez playing together again had been a terrific idea. But Dylan was never really interested again until 1984, when he once more invited Joan on a European tour that he was sharing with Carlos Santana. For her to accept the invitation, because tickets were not selling well and they needed a lure, the promoter made promises to Baez that came to nothing: the duets with Dylan didn't happen and her participation was reduced to a warm-up act. Angry and feeling manipulated once more, she left halfway through the tour.

These days Baez speaks fondly of Dylan in her interviews, but she is clear. You take away as much peace as you leave behind, Bobby.

When Tom Waits collided with Rickie Lee Jones in the Los Angeles of 1977, it was like twin souls meeting. Their love of beat poetry and jazz united Tom, who had already released several albums at that time and was struggling to make a living from music, and Rickie Lee, who, still unknown, had been invited to sing a couple of songs in a friend's show at the famous Troubadour in Los Angeles that summer.

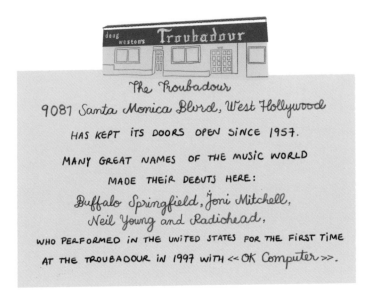

The Troubadour

9081 Santa Monica Blvd, West Hollywood

HAS KEPT ITS DOORS OPEN SINCE 1957.

MANY GREAT NAMES OF THE MUSIC WORLD
MADE THEIR DEBUTS HERE:

Buffalo Springfield, Joni Mitchell,
Neil Young and Radiohead,

WHO PERFORMED IN THE UNITED STATES FOR THE FIRST TIME
AT THE TROUBADOUR IN 1997 WITH << OK Computer >>.

Although they had a great deal in common, Tom and Rickie Lee came from very different places. Tom was an ordinary middle-class guy who had lived for nine years in the Tropicana Inn, a modest motel in Los Angeles through which had also hosted the likes of Jim Morrison, Stevie Nicks, Joan Jett and The Ramones, penniless musicians who played for peanuts in the nearby dens and concert rooms of West Hollywood.

Tom lived in a rather unusual way. He had a piano in the kitchen of his small apartment in the Tropicana on which he composed at night, while he spent a large part of the day sleeping.

Around 1975, Rickie Lee Jones was a twenty-one-year-old go-getter, a free spirit and bohemian who, at the age of fourteen, had made herself independent from her family, a rootless clan of vaudeville actors who lived a nomadic existence travelling the country. Around that time, she was working as a waitress to make ends meet and performing occasionally. It was not unusual for her to have to sleep outside under the stars and the gigantic Hollywood sign.

By the end of 1977, Tom and Rickie Lee were inseparable, along with their good friend Chuck E. Weiss, a musician who was temporarily washing-up at The Troubadour. Partying, alcohol, drugs ... they were three nocturnal romantic vagabonds who were moved by the musical *West Side Story* while living on the edge, haunted like something out of a poem by Bukowski.

MY FAVOURITE RECORD BY Tom Waits is →
<< Blue Valentine >>.
THE OPENING SONG OF THE LP IS A VERSION OF
<< S O M E W H E R E >>,
ONE OF Leonard Berstein's SONGS
FOR THE MUSICAL << West Side Story >>.
ON THE ALBUM COVER,
Rickie Lee Jones and Chuck E. Weiss
ARE IN A 24-HOUR GAS STATION WITH THEIR 1964 THUNDERBIRD.

Shortly afterwards, Rickie Lee Jones began to attract the notice of record labels. When she released her first album, *Rickie Lee Jones*, she was an instant sensation, even though the current fashion on the radio favoured disco and new wave. Her jazz-flavoured single, 'Chuck E's in Love', inspired by her great friend Weiss, took her into the top five of sales lists and won the Grammy for Best New Artist.

THE PRESS SURRENDERED TO HER PERSONAL STYLE: *berets, mittens and vintage clothes.* THAT SAME YEAR, SHE WAS ON THE COVER OF THE MAGAZINE *Rolling Stone.*

In 1979 Rickie Lee Jones became the superstar her boyfriend had still not managed to become. However, the unstable life she had lived until then made her too vulnerable to success, and she found refuge in heroin. All this damaged her relationship with Tom Waits, who was unable to handle the success and addictions towards which his problematic girlfriend dragged him.

At the end of 1979 they broke up. Tom moved to New York and went into treatment for drug addiction.

This was too much for one year. Exhausted and broken-hearted, Rickie Lee composed her new and successful album, *Pirates* (1981), a posthumous testament to her relationship with Waits.

SMASH HIT ! << We Belong Together >>.

Her problems with drug use, her difficult recovery, the later death of her father and the birth of her daughter interrupted her career for almost a decade. She has since picked it up again and she still records and tours, but she has never again achieved such resounding success.

For Waits, his break-up with Jones was symptomatic of a need for change that was guided by Kathleen Brennan, a screenwriter he met filming *One from the Heart*, by Francis Ford Coppola, for which Waits composed the soundtrack and in which he had a small role.

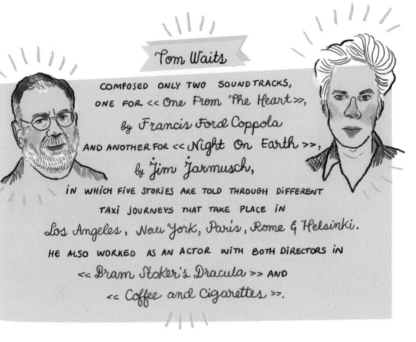

Tom Waits

COMPOSED ONLY TWO SOUNDTRACKS, ONE FOR << *One From The Heart* >>, by Francis Ford Coppola AND ANOTHER FOR << *Night On Earth* >>, by Jim Jarmusch, IN WHICH FIVE STORIES ARE TOLD THROUGH DIFFERENT TAXI JOURNEYS THAT TAKE PLACE IN Los Angeles, New York, Paris, Rome & Helsinki. HE ALSO WORKED AS AN ACTOR WITH BOTH DIRECTORS IN << *Bram Stoker's Dracula* >> AND << *Coffee and Cigarettes* >>.

Brennan, apart from working as a story analyst at Zoetrope Studios, Coppola's production company, was a versatile artist who encouraged Waits to explore new musical forms, moving away from his influences that were more oriented towards jazz and blues.

She also had a remarkable record collection and was the person who introduced him to the records of Captain Beefheart, a major influence on Tom Waits' career.

Tom and Kathleen married in 1980 and had three children. She became Waits' chief inspiration and together they co-wrote most of Waits' songs from that time on.

CORIN TUCKER & CARRIE BROWNSTEIN
(1992-1996)

Corin Tucker and Carrie Brownstein met on the music scene of the Washington underground punk feminist movement, Riot Grrrl, in 1992.

PARIS

THE BANDS OF

Riot Grrrl

WERE

≈ *women only* ≈

AND THEY DEALT WITH THEMES SUCH AS SEXUAL ABUSE, RAPE,
RACISM, MACHISMO, THE PATRIARCHY AND THE EMPOWERMENT
OF WOMEN.

THIS MOVEMENT INCLUDED

power *feminism*

Bikini Kill *Heavens to Betsy*

Let's smash PATRIARCHY together!

self love I fight like a girl!

Bratmobile *Excuse 17*

On leaving high school, Carrie Brownstein attended Evergreen State College,
where she met Corin Tucker. Carrie formed the band Excuse 17, which often
organised joint tours with Corin's group, Heavens to Betsy.

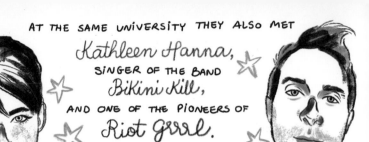

AT THE SAME UNIVERSITY THEY ALSO MET

Kathleen Hanna,
SINGER OF THE BAND
Bikini Kill,
AND ONE OF THE PIONEERS OF
Riot grrrl.
AFTER THAT
KATHLEEN FORMED *Le Tigre*
AND LATER *The Julie Ruin.*

Kathleen Hanna IS THE PARTNER OF *Adam Horovitz,*
OF THE HIP-HOP BAND
The Beastie Boys.

THEIR RELATIONSHIP BEGAN IN 1997
AND THEY MARRIED IN 2006.

Heavens to Betsy recorded their first and only album, *Calculated*, in 1993 and then the band dissolved. Corin and Carrie got along well, fell in love and decided to form the group Sleater-Kinney, which is named after a motorway exit in Washington. Although the band was initially begun as a parallel project for both of them, it soon took all their attention, especially when Excuse 17 fell apart in 1995.

Sleater-Kinney recorded its first album in 1994, during a trip to Australia to celebrate Corin's graduation. They always used temporary drummers until Janet Weiss joined the band in 1997.

With their second LP, *Call the Doctor* (1996), Sleater-Kinney got even better reviews than with their debut album.

The music magazine *Spin* published a transgressive article in which it openly stated Carrie Brownstein's bisexuality and her relationship with Corin. Carrie's father, who had brought her up after separating from his wife, admitted his own homosexuality to her almost at the same time as his daughter's bisexuality was revealed through this article.

Their third album, *Dig Me Out* (1997), established them as a band of the nineties. Among their songs was the sincere 'One More Hour', in which a broken-hearted Corin Tucker spoke of her breakup with Carrie Brownstein, who had apparently met another girl.

« One More Hour », IN A SNUG DIALOGUE TYPICAL OF Sleater-Kinney, CONSISTED OF AN IMPLORING CORIN AND A STOICAL CARRIE.

In spite of their personal break-up, Sleater-Kinney continued until 2006. The group then gave itself a big break until 2015, when it released *No Cities to Love*.

Corin Tucker
MARRIED DIRECTOR Lance Bangs IN 2002
AND HAD TWO CHILDREN WITH HIM. LANCE HAS MADE
MUSIC VIDEOS FOR

Sonic Youth
Pavement
The White Stripes
Belle & Sebastian
Arcade Fire
Death Cab for Cutie

FOR HER PART,
Carrie Brownstein
HAS HAD SUCCESSES ON AMERICAN TELEVISION IN SERIES SUCH AS
« Portlandia » and « Transparent ».

JOHN LENNON & YOKO ONO
(1966–1980)

Around 1966 John Lennon
met Yoko Ono in the Indica Gallery
in London, where she was putting
together an exhibition. Yoko
belonged to Fluxus, a community
of avant-garde conceptual artists
working both in Europe and the
United States in the sixties.

Lennon was impressed by an installation by Yoko that involved going up a wooden ladder and holding an enormous spyglass through which you could read a small inscription on the ceiling that said, 'Yes!'

They became friends, and in 1967 Lennon funded her first solo exhibition in London's Lisson Gallery.

At the beginning of 1968, The Beatles visited India along with their wives, girlfriends, assistants and various journalists to learn about transcendental meditation with the Maharishi Mahesh Yogi. It was a very productive experience for the band, and they composed the songs for their new record, *The White Album*, there.

Lennon and Harrison
WERE THE ONES WHO STAYED THERE LONGEST,
UNTIL THEY LEFT SUDDENLY DUE TO
ECONOMIC DISAGREEMENTS AND BECAUSE OF
INAPPROPRIATE BEHAVIOUR BY THE

MAHARISHI
TOWARDS THE WOMEN.
AMONG OTHER SONGS, JOHN COMPOSED
<< *Julia* >>,
WHICH INCLUDES THE PHRASE << *Ocean child calls me* >>
IN REFERENCE TO THE NAME
Yoko,
WHICH IN JAPANESE MEANS 'CHILD OF THE OCEAN'.

On his return to London, while his wife was visiting Greece, John invited Yoko to move into his house to record what would be the experimental album *Two Virgins* (1968). On her return, Cynthia Lennon could see that her marriage was broken. They were divorced a year later.

Yoko and John married in Gibraltar in 1969 and spent their honeymoon in Amsterdam, in the Hilton Hotel, where they shut themselves up in room 702 for a week as a protest against the Vietnam War.

The couple, dressed in pyjamas and lying in bed with a guitar, surrounded by flowers and banners, opened their room to the press for twelve hours a day to discuss peace. The performance of the two artists passed into history under the name *Bed-In for Peace*.

THE TRACK
<< *The Ballad of John and Yoko* >>
IS ABOUT THIS PERIOD. THE DOCUMENTARY
<< *Bed Peace* >>
TELLS US ABOUT THE BED-IN IN AMSTERDAM AND
IS AVAILABLE ON YOUTUBE.

Yoko and John tried to repeat the event in the United States, but the authorities would not allow it. Then they opted to hold it in the Queen Elizabeth Hotel in Montreal, where they recorded the famous song 'Give Peace a Chance' along with dozens of reporters and well-known figures, such as Allen Ginsberg and Petula Clark. By 1970, Yoko and John were inseparable and the musician left The Beatles.

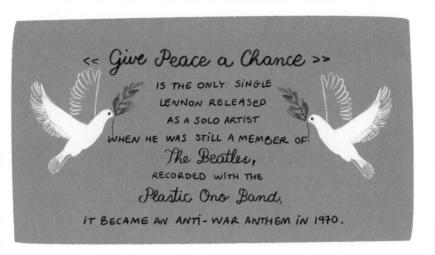

<< *Give Peace a Chance* >> IS THE ONLY SINGLE LENNON RELEASED AS A SOLO ARTIST WHEN HE WAS STILL A MEMBER OF *The Beatles*, RECORDED WITH THE *Plastic Ono Band*, IT BECAME AN ANTI-WAR ANTHEM IN 1970.

After breaking with his historic group, John moved to New York with Yoko. In September 1971, Lennon released *Imagine*, an album coproduced with Yoko and Phil Spector.

THE SIMPLE << *Imagine* >> WAS NUMBER ONE AND NUMBER THREE IN THE UK AND THE US RESPECTIVELY. IN 1972, THEY RELEASED THE 81-MINUTE FILM << I M A G I N E >>, WITH SCENES OF JOHN AND YOKO AT HOME PLAYING TOGETHER AT THEIR WHITE PIANO. OTHER APPEARANCES IN THE FILM WERE MADE BY:

Andy Warhol,
Fred Astaire
AND *George Harrison.*

However, all was not well with the couple. John was facing an ongoing threat of deportation for charges of drug possession, and Yoko was struggling with the separation from her daughter from a previous marriage. The father had obtained custody of the minor and disappeared with her in 1971. Yoko was not to see her again until 1998.

The couple went through a separation in 1973. Yoko focused on her solo career and John lived between Los Angeles and New York with his new girlfriend, his assistant May Pang, with whom he spent a year and a half before getting back together with Yoko. After his 'lost weekend' (as John referred to this affair), Yoko gave birth to their son, Sean Lennon, in 1975.

Sean Lennon

FOLLOWED IN HIS PARENTS' FOOTSTEPS
AND FORMED THE DUO
The Ghost of a Saber Tooth Tiger
WITH HIS PARTNER
Charlotte Kemp Muhl.

After Sean's birth, Lennon decided to take a five-year break from his music career and devote himself to caring for his family. In 1980 he released *Double Fantasy*, the final album published in his lifetime before he was shot and killed by a fan at the main entrance of the Dakota building, where he lived.

THE

Dakota

BUILDING

on the corner of 72nd Street and Central Park West,
on the Upper West Side of New York,
WAS BUILT IN 1884. IT IS ONE OF MANHATTAN'S MOST
PRESTIGIOUS RESIDENTIAL BUILDINGS, AND HAS BEEN
HOME TO FIGURES SUCH AS

Lauren Bacall, Judy Garland and Boris Karloff,
AS WELL AS
John Lennon.
IN
Roman Polanski's
<< Rosemary's Baby >>,
THE EXTERIOR OF THE DAKOTA WAS FILMED
TO REPRESENT
The Bramford,
THE HOME OF THE CHARACTERS IN THE FILM.

Yoko Ono scattered his ashes in Central Park, where later the Strawberry Fields Memorial was created in Lennon's memory. In 1984 a posthumous album, *Milk and Honey*, was released, which included the songs recorded for *Double Fantasy* and later discarded.

PATTI SMITH & FRED «Sonic» SMITH

(end of 1970s – 1994)

Patti Smith arrived in New York in 1967, aged twenty, with a few clothes and a book of Rimbaud poems. She left behind her family, her work in a factory and a daughter to an unknown father, whom she gave up for adoption.

PATTI HAS BEEN A GREAT READER SINCE CHILDHOOD. AS A RATHER SICKLY CHILD, SHE TOOK REFUGE IN BOOKS. A GREAT ADMIRER OF

Charles Baudelaire
&
William Blake,

AFTER SUFFERING FROM SCARLET FEVER SHE CALLED ON HER HALLUCINATIONS TO WRITE HER FIRST POEMS.

She began to work in a bookshop, where she met the photographer Robert Mapplethorpe, her first great love and one of the most important people in her life. They scraped by, living in room 1017 of the Chelsea Hotel, and hanging out in Max's Kansas City and CBGB. Robert was originally a fine arts student, and it was Patti who encouraged him to give up his paintbrushes and start taking photos. Robert, in return, gave her the idea of turning her poems into songs. However, the couple were not compatible sexually, though Robert did not admit to being gay. They broke up, but remained friends until Robert's death from AIDS in 1989.

In the early seventies Patti had a tortuous affair with a married man in an open relationship, the American playwright Sam Shepard, who broke her heart.

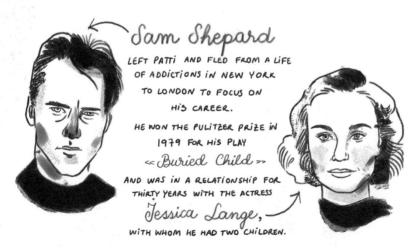

Sam Shepard

LEFT PATTI AND FLED FROM A LIFE OF ADDICTIONS IN NEW YORK TO LONDON TO FOCUS ON HIS CAREER.

HE WON THE PULITZER PRIZE IN 1979 FOR HIS PLAY

<< Buried Child >>

AND WAS IN A RELATIONSHIP FOR THIRTY YEARS WITH THE ACTRESS

Jessica Lange,

WITH WHOM HE HAD TWO CHILDREN.

In 1973, Smith began a relationship with Allen Lanier, keyboard player of the band Blue Öyster Cult, with whom she spent eight years. Patti contributed to the lyrics of the band's songs, such as 'Debbie Denise', 'Career of Evil' and 'The Revenge of Vera Gemini', for which she also recorded the vocals. In these years, as well as publishing two books of poems, she contributed articles to *Rolling Stone* and *Cream*.

In 1975 she formed a band with guitarist Lenny Kaye and finally released her first album, *Horses*, produced by John Cale, with the legendary androgynous portrait by Robert Mapplethorpe on the cover.

« H O R S E S »

IS THE FIRST ART PUNK ALBUM, A MIX
OF PUNK ROCK AND SPOKEN WORD. THE RECORD BEGINS
WITH A COVER OF
« *Gloria* »,
by
Van Morrison.
WITH HER PARTNER *Allen Lanier*, PATTI WROTE
« *Elegie* » & « *Kimberly* ».

Patti Smith released three more records: *Radio Ethiopia*, *Easter* and *Wave*. In spite of the success of her single 'Because the Night', co-written with Bruce Springsteen, she dissolved her band in 1979 and disappeared from the scene.

At the end of the seventies, Patti began a relationship with Fred 'Sonic' Smith, the guitarist from the Detroit band MC5.

IN HER ALBUM << *Wave* >> (1979), SHE DEDICATES << *Dancing Barefoot* >> & << *Frederick* >> TO FRED.

The couple married in 1980. Patti moved to Detroit and gave up music to devote herself to bringing up their two children.

IN 2009, HER SON JACKSON MARRIED *Meg White*, THE DRUMMER OF *The White Stripes*, A BAND SHE SET UP WITH HER FORMER HUSBAND *Jack White*, WHOM SHE DIVORCED IN 2000. JACK REBUILT HIS LIFE WITH THE MODEL AND NOW SINGER *Karen Elson*. JACK AND MEGAN WHITE DIVORCED THEIR RESPECTIVE SPOUSES IN 2013.

Patti came out of her musical retirement sporadically. In 1988, she released *Dream of Life*, recorded, with her husband on guitar, during the last few months of Mapplethorpe's life. In 1994, Fred 'Sonic' Smith also died, from a heart attack, and a year later, her brother, from a stroke. Patti was devastated.

ANOTHER TRAGIC STORY IS THAT OF ONE OF SPAIN'S MOST INTERESTING COUPLES, *Eduardo Benavente* & *Ana Curra*, of PARALISIS PERMANENTE, WHICH ENDED WITH A CAR CRASH ON THE WAY BACK FROM A GIG IN ZARAGOZA. ANA CURRA WAS HOSPITALISED, BUT EDUARDO DIED IN THE ACCIDENT.

THEIR ONLY ALBUM, << E L A C T O >> (1992), IS A PUNK GEM.

Patti moved back to New York. Her friends Michael Stipe and Allen Ginsberg were waiting for her, and they began to encourage her to go back to her music. Her friend Bob Dylan convinced her to rejoin her band and invited her on his 1995 tour, which was recorded in Michael Stipe's book of photographs *Two Times Intro: On the Road with Patti Smith*.

Patti's true comeback was marked by the release of her album *Gone Again* in 1996, and since then she has not stopped. Today, she is considered an icon of music history.

After going out together for almost a year, Ben Gibbard, frontman of Death Cab for Cutie and Postal Service, proposed to Zooey Deschanel, actress and singer in She & Him.

They had been introduced by their manager around 2008. She had already caught Ben's eye when he saw her on screen. He had idealised her and in an interview with *New York Magazine*, he said that he found it mind-blowing that she should even be interested in talking to him.

AT A FUNDRAISER ORGANISED BY BARACK OBAMA THAT YEAR, *Zooey & Ben* SANG « *All I Have to Do Is Dream* » *by The Everly Brothers,* ONE OF THE FIRST TEN BANDS INDUCTED INTO THE *Rock & Roll Hall of Fame.* THIS SONG, RELEASED IN 1958, HAD ON ITS B-SIDE « *Claudette* », WHICH WAS WRITTEN BY *Roy Orbison.*

Ben was experiencing a period of change. The shy, chubby singer released his sixth studio album with Death Cab for Cutie, *Narrow Stairs*, a turning point in his professional career and in his way of writing. After its release, the sensitive songwriter of break-ups and heartbreaks decided that there was too much negativity in his life and that he had channelled it all into that album.

<< *The Ice is Getting Thinner* >> is one of my favourite songs on this record. *Ben Gibbard* has written about the end of love on many occasions, such as in << *A Lack of Color* >>, << *Title and Registration* >> and << *Tiny Vessels* >>.

At the end of 2008, Ben went on a diet, stopped drinking, took up running and got himself a girlfriend. Zooey and Ben were the indie couple of the moment. They regularly went on stage at each other's concerts to sing a duet, doing retro-style covers of songs such as 'I'll Never Find Another You' by The Seekers.

Zooey was in a good place in her life. She and Ben married in Seattle on 19 September 2009. While preparing for her wedding, she finished recording *Volume II* with She & Him, and the film that established her as an indie muse, *(500) Days of Summer*, had just come out. Although the leader of Death Cab for Cutie was going through a personal crisis at the time, there had been no stopping Zooey.

IN << (500) *Days of Summer* >>
THE MUSIC PLAYS A SIGNIFICANT ROLE IN THE NARRATIVE.
THE SOUNDTRACK WAS CHOSEN WITH FINE TASTE, WITH SONGS BY
The Smiths, Feist and Pixies.

After a marriage of just three years, Ben and Zooey separated by mutual consent. Without many explanations, they divorced officially in 2012. Death Cab for Cutie released its album *Keys and Codes* in 2011, followed by *Kintsugi* in 2015.

I HAVE NO IDEA WHETHER THE FLEETING APPEARENCE OF ZOOEY IN HIS LIFE, A LACK OF INSPIRATION OR THE DEPARTURE OF HIS GUITARIST AND CO-WRITER

Chris Walla

IN 2013 WERE TO BLAME, OR WHETHER MARATHONS WERE TAKING ALL HIS ENERGY, BUT I'VE BEEN DISAPPOINTED BY BEN'S MOST RECENT RECORDS. I NEED TO LOOK FOR ANOTHER FAVOURITE GROUP.

LEONARD COHEN & JONI MITCHELL & GRAHAM NASH
(1967-1968) (1969-1971)

Leonard Cohen met Joni Mitchell at the 1967 Newport Folk Festival. His friend, singer Judy Collins, introduced them backstage of one of the sets. Leonard, aged thirty-three, had just released his first album, *Songs of Leonard Cohen*, and had published several poetry books. Joni Mitchell, who was nine years younger, was yet to release a record, but was already composing for other artists.

Judy Collins

RECORDED SONGS BY COHEN AND MITCHELL BEFORE THEIR OWN AUTHORS DID. COLLINS HAD ALREADY POPULARISED THE LEGENDARY *Suzanne*, WHICH FEATURED IN LEONARD'S DEBUT ALBUM, ON HER ALBUM *In my life* A YEAR EARLIER.

AND HER VERSION OF *Both Sides Now*, BY *Joni Mitchell*, WAS HER GREAT INTERNATIONAL SUCCESS. JONI RECORDED IT TWO YEARS LATER, IN 1969, FOR HER ALBUM *Clouds*. AROUND THAT TIME JUDY COLLINS WAS THE GIRLFRIEND OF *Stephen Stills*, OF *Crosby, Stills & Nash*. AFTER A RELATIONSHIP OF TWO YEARS, THEY SPLIT UP AND STILLS WROTE *Suite: Judy Blue Eyes* ABOUT THEIR BREAK-UP, WHICH APPEARED ON THE BAND'S DEBUT ALBUM IN 1969.

Leonard Cohen, disappointed by his limited success as a writer, had just left the peaceful hippie village where he'd been living on the Greek island of Hydra to try his luck as a singer-songwriter in the United States. For her part, Joni carried the burden of a divorce and a secret: a hidden pregnancy and a baby given away for adoption. They did, however, have a great deal in common. Both were Canadian, and both were successful in the late seventies on the folk scene. They shared an intense love affair, which ended just a few months later, in 1968.

THE RELATIONSHIP WITH COHEN HAD AN INSPIRATIONAL EFFECT ON JONI MITCHELL'S WRITING. SHE ADMIRED HIM DEEPLY. << Rainy Night House >> IS A SONG OF FAREWELL THAT SHE DEDICATED TO HIM.

HOTEL
CHELSEA

AT THAT TIME
Leonard Cohen
WAS LIVING IN ROOM 424 OF THE

Hotel Chelsea,

WHICH WAS MORE FAMOUS THAN HE WAS.
BUILT IN 1883 ITS FOUR HUNDRED ROOMS WERE
HOME FOR LONG PERIODS TO MANY
ARTISTS AND INTELLECTUALS, WHO TURNED IT INTO A
NEW YORK BOHEMIAN HAUNT:

Bukowski, Jackson Pollock, Arthur Miller,
William S. Burroughs, Stanley Kubrick,
Dennis Hopper, Patti Smith, Robert Crumb,
Dee Dee Ramone, Nico and more.

IT WAS HERE THAT *Dylan Thomas* DRANK HIMSELF
TO DEATH AND, YEARS LATER, *Sid Vicious* ALLEGEDLY STABBED
HIS GIRLFRIEND *Nancy Spungen* TO DEATH.

IN THE SIXTIES IT BECAME A RESIDENCE FOR THE
BOHEMIAN ELITE, WITH TENANTS SUCH AS
Jimi Hendrix, The Grateful Dead,
Bob Dylan and Leonard Cohen.

Andy Warhol FILMED «*Chelsea Girls*» HERE IN 1966.
AND HERE *Lou Reed* WROTE «*Chelsea Girls*»
Jefferson Airplane, «*Third Week in Chelsea*»
and Joni Mitchell, «*Chelsea Morning*»

ON 1 AUGUST 2011 THE HOTEL
STOPPED TAKING BOOKINGS.

One spring day in 1968, Leonard Cohen was returning to the Chelsea in the early hours of the morning from the White Horse Tavern, an iconic dive in Greenwich Village. He took the lift and a twenty-five-year-old singer from Texas, Janis Joplin, who lived in room 411, got in. Intrigued by her eccentric appearance, Leonard Cohen began a conversation as best he could that ended up in the song 'Chelsea Hotel', which recounts the sexual encounter between the two.

Janis Joplin

DIED OF A HEROIN OVERDOSE ON 4 OCTOBER 1970. JUST A FEW MONTHS LATER, << Me and Bobby McGee >>, WHICH SHE HAD RECORDED A FEW DAYS BEFORE SHE DIED, BECAME HER ONLY NUMBER ONE SINGLE. AT THE BEGINNING OF 1971, MOVED BY HER DEATH, LEONARD WROTE HIS FIRST LINES OF << Chelsea Hotel >> ON A NAPKIN IN A MIAMI BAR. HE DID NOT RECORD IT UNTIL 1974, FOR HIS ALBUM << New Skin for the Old Ceremony >>.

At the end of the sixties, Graham Nash left behind his band The Hollies, and his marriage in the UK for California, Crosby, Stills & Nash and Joni Mitchell.

He had met Joni in Canada a few months earlier, on a tour with The Hollies. After the concert, they were introduced at a private party and felt an instant connection. So much so that they spent the night together in Joni's room at The Château Laurier after a solo rendition of fifteen songs for the exclusive delight of Nash. In love, he returned to the UK, but not to stay.

Graham went to live with Joni in Laurel Canyon, Los Angeles. Their life together was idyllic, in a 1930s house with wooden floors, decorated with a piano, guitars and Joni's paintings; and a pair of cats sunbathing in the garden. They divided up the rooms to compose in this inspiring atmosphere.

One day, on the way back from having breakfast in a deli, Joni bought a simple vase. When they got home, she put flowers from the garden in it while Graham composed the first lines of 'Our House', to capture the moment. Crosby, Stills, Nash & Young (as they were now called) recorded it for *Déjà Vu* (1970), their highest-selling album.

For her part, Joni composed 'Willy', as Graham was known to his friends. The song appears on her album *Ladies of the Canyon* (1970).

After three years together, Joni began to cut herself off and went into a personal crisis. One day, Graham received a telegram from Europe in which Joni brought their relationship to an end.

<< If you hold sand too tightly in your hand, it will run through your fingers.
Love, Joan. >>

In 1971, Graham Nash released *Songs for Beginners*, his first solo album, including songs such as 'I Used to Be a King' and 'Sleep Song', in which, still in love with Joni, he writes about their break-up and about how much he misses her. In the same year, Joni released *Blue*, her most introspective, honest and personal work. Her very intimate lyrics give us clues as to the problems with Nash and the paradox of being human: that we get tired of being loved.

A MASTERPIECE: << A Case of You >> is AN ODE TO THE MOST TOXIC DESIRE AND PASSION iN WHiCH MiTCHELL OPENLY DiSPLAYS HER VULNERABiLiTY.

COURTNEY LOVE & KURT COBAIN
(1990-1994)

Kurt Cobain and Courtney Love met at a Nirvana gig in Portland's Satyricon club in 1990. Minutes before the concert started, Courtney bumped into Kurt and she told him that he looked like Dave Pirner of Soul Asylum. He grabbed her round the waist and they ended up in a mock struggle on the floor in front of a jukebox, on which a song by Living Colour was playing.

Satyricon,

THE CBGB OF THE WEST COAST, OPENED IN 1983
IN PORTLAND, OREGON. MANY FAMOUS BANDS PASSED THROUGH
THE NIGHTCLUB, INCLUDING *Mudhoney, Nirvana, Pavement,
Sleater-Kinney, Spoon and Green Day.*
IT WAS ALSO HERE THAT THE
Foo Fighters
PERFORMED FOR THE VERY FIRST TIME.

Nirvana had just released *Bleach* (1989) on the independent label Sub Pop. That same year, Courtney Love formed Hole while earning her living as a stripper in Los Angeles, and had a brief marriage that lasted a few months with transvestite James Moreland, vocalist of The Leaving Trains.

LOSER

Sub Pop

IS AN INDEPENDENT RECORD LABEL SET UP IN Seattle, Washington IN 1986. IT WAS THE FIRST LABEL TO SIGN UP Nirvana, Soundgarden and Mudhoney AND IT PROMOTED THE EMERGING GRUNGE SCENE. IT NOW BELONGS TO THE GIANT WARNER MUSIC GROUP, WHICH HAS A 49 PER CENT STAKE, AND INCLUDES IN ITS POOL Beach House, Band Of Horses, Goat and Father John Misty.

Kurt and Courtney were not to see each other again until a year later, when they were introduced at an L7 and Butthole Surfers concert in Los Angeles.

Nirvana decided to sign up with a bigger label, DGC Records, and they released the legendary *Nevermind* (1991) which, with sales of more than thirty million copies, managed to knock Michael Jackson's *Dangerous* off the top spot, bringing 'Seattle sound' worldwide popularity.

FOR *Nevermind*

Dave Grohl

JOINED NIRVANA ON DRUMS.
THE PHOTO ON THE COVER WAS IMMORTALISED BY
Kirk Weddle, WHO PAID FRIENDS $200
TO USE THEIR BABY, *Spencer Elden*,
BORN IN 1991, AS A MODEL. IN 2001 SPENCER
POSED AGAIN TO RECREATE THE ALBUM COVER PHOTO FOR
ROLLING STONE ON THE TENTH ANNIVERSARY OF THE ALBUM,
AND HE DID THE SAME AGAIN IN 2008 AND 2016.

At the same time, Hole released *Pretty on the Inside* with Caroline Records, produced by Kim Gordon of Sonic Youth. The two artists had met when Hole was opening for Sonic Youth on the promotional tour for *Goo* at the legendary Whisky a Go Go club on Sunset Boulevard in 1990. Following the tour, Courtney had written to Kim to ask her if she would produce their record. She agreed, and the record was well-received by critics and the public alike. During that year Courtney had a brief love affair with Billy Corgan of The Smashing Pumpkins.

By the end of 1991, Love and Cobain began a relationship that made them inseparable and turned them into *the* grunge couple. Both consumed large quantities of drugs. Although Kurt's first experience of heroin had been in 1986, it was not until 1990 that he became an addict.

Courtney and Kurt married quietly at Waikiki Beach, Hawaii, on 24 February 1992. The groom wore flannel pyjamas. The bride wore a white satin and lace dress that had once belonged to actress Frances Farmer, whose problematic and combative personality inspired Kurt to write the song 'Frances Farmer Will Have Her Revenge on Seattle', which appears on Nirvana's album *In Utero* (1993).

Frances Farmer (1907 - 1970)

WAS A CLASSICAL HOLLYWOOD ACTRESS BORN IN SEATTLE, WHO TOOK ON THE WORLD AND THE INDUSTRY WITH HER REBELLIOUSNESS. HER NONCONFORMIST NATURE, THE OPPRESSIVE FIGURE OF HER MOTHER AND THE ATMOSPHERE OF HOLLYWOOD LED HER INTO ALCOHOLISM, DRUG ADDICTION AND COMMITTAL FOR YEARS TO A PSYCHIATRIC HOSPITAL WHERE SHE WAS SUBJECTED TO ELECTROSHOCK THERAPY, RAPED BY NURSES AND DESIGNATED FOR A LOBOTOMY TO DESTROY HER IRREPRESSIBLE NATURE. SHE FINALLY LEFT THE HOSPITAL AND WANDERED THROUGH LIFE LIKE A ZOMBIE, A SHADOW OF WHAT SHE HAD BEEN. KURT COBAIN IDENTIFIED FRANCES' PERSONALITY WITH THAT OF

Courtney Love.

Courtney Love was already three months pregnant with Frances Bean Cobain at the time of their wedding. Both Courtney and Kurt were keen to come off drugs so as not to harm their baby. In 1992, in an interview with *Vanity Fair*, Love admitted to having used heroin before she realised that she was pregnant. There was a great fuss about whether or not this would cause Frances to be born addicted. Social services took the couple to court, alleging that their drug problem rendered them incapable of functioning as parents. The couple finally won custody, with regular visits from social workers to supervise the situation.

AN ULTRASOUND OF FRANCES WAS INCLUDED ON THE COVER OF THE SINGLE << *Lithium* >>, FROM << *In Utero* >>.

Although the reception of *In Utero* (1993) was generally good, sales were not as big as with *Nevermind*, so Nirvana accepted an offer from MTV to take part in an acoustic concert. After its recording, they released *MTV Unplugged* in New York, which had better sales than *In Utero*.

In February 1994, when Nirvana were on tour in Europe, Kurt spent a few days with Courtney in Rome. One morning, Love woke up to find her husband unconscious from an overdose of tranquillisers mixed with champagne. Kurt had left a suicide note.

Cobain returned to Seattle and was hospitalised for a week, but his mental and emotional state worsened. Tormented by his troubled mind and drug abuse, after repeated suicide attempts, admissions into and escapes from rehab centres, he ended his life on 5 April 1994 with a shot to the head in his Seattle home. He became known as the voice of Generation X.

IN THE DAYS OF GRUNGE AND CHECKED SHIRTS, THERE WAS ONE MUSICIAN (WHO ALSO DIED IN TRAGIC CIRCUMSTANCES) WHO OFFERED THE PUBLIC AN ALTERNATIVE OF DELICATE MELODIES AND GREAT AESTHETIC SENSITIVITY.

JEFF BUCKLEY

DROWNED BY ACCIDENT IN THE MISSISSIPPI AT THE AGE OF THIRTY, IN 1997. HIS GIRLFRIEND Joan Wasser, WHO HAD BEGUN HER CAREER AS A VIOLINIST, HAD BEEN IN A RELATIONSHIP WITH HIM FOR THREE YEARS.

TODAY SHE IS THE SOUL OF THE BAND Joan As Police Woman.

Hole released their most commercial album and greatest success, *Live Through This* (1994), just a week after Kurt Cobain's death. Controversy surrounded this release, since it was rumoured that Cobain had had a lot more to do with its composition than Courtney Love herself.

Love has continued to struggle with her addictions for the rest of her life. In 1996 she came off drugs at the request of director Milos Forman, who wanted her to appear in *The People vs. Larry Flint*. However, in 2004, at the age of forty, she attempted suicide in her Manhattan apartment. After being arrested repeatedly for drug use and violation of probation conditions, she was sentenced to six months of rehab. Courtney Love claims to have been drug free since 2007.

<< *Kurt Cobain : Montage Of Heck* >> IS A DOCUMENTARY ABOUT THE LIFE OF NIRVANA'S FRONT MAN, FIRST SHOWN AT SUNDANCE AND ON HBO IN 2015. THE FILM'S CO-EXECUTIVE PRODUCER WAS *Frances Bean Cobain*.

TINA & IKE TURNER
(1958 - 1976)

In 1957 Kings of Rhythm, the rock and roll band formed by Ike Turner in the late forties, was among the most popular in the nightlife of St Louis, Missouri. Tina Turner, then known as Anna Mae Bullock, had just moved to the city and became obsessed with joining the band after seeing them perform in the Club DeLisa.

Accompanied by her sister, Tina followed them to every concert they gave. One night, in the Club Manhattan, she asked Ike to let her sing on stage and, although he didn't refuse, he pretended not to notice. Tina got fed up, grabbed a microphone in the middle of the performance and sang the BB King song that Kings of Rhythm were playing at the time.

Ike, who had worked as a talent scout for record labels some years before, was impressed.

Tina

BEGAN GOING OUT WITH Raymond Hill, THE Kings of Rhythm SAXOPHONIST, WITH WHOM SHE HAD HER SON Raymond Craig IN 1958, BUT THE RELATIONSHIP ENDED AFTER A HUGE ROW. TINA MOVED WITH THE CHILD INTO IKE'S HOUSE, AND IKE LATER LEGALLY ADOPTED HIM. RAYMOND HILL LEFT THE BAND.

To begin with, there was no attraction between Ike and Tina; they loved each other like brother and sister. When Tina moved into his house, Ike began to give her music and singing lessons. Ike later claimed to have been married thirteen times (the actual number was never verified), but then, although aged only thirty, he was married to his fifth wife, Lorraine Taylor, with whom he had two children.

Ike believed that Tina, still known at that time by the nickname Little Ann, was not ready to be the group's soloist and he had chosen another singer to front the Kings of Rhythm, for whom he had written 'A Fool in Love' (1959). On the day of the recording the singer didn't turn up, so Ike called on Tina, who was the band's back-up singer, to record the demo.

They signed up with Sue Records and 'A Fool in Love' became a hit. Ike renamed Little Ann, who was by that time his lover, Tina Turner, and so the duo Ike & Tina Turner, R&B stars of the sixties, was born.

Ike & Tina Turner's TV DEBUT WAS ON THE SHOW American Bandstand, IN OCTOBER 1960. TINA WAS PREGNANT AT THE TIME WITH HER FIRST SON WITH IKE.

Ike and Tina married in Tijuana in 1962, in spite of the fact that he was legally married to another woman. However, their relationship would be one marked by abuse, fighting and beatings fuelled by drugs and alcohol.

Whitney Houston & Bobby Brown

MARRIED IN 1992 AND THEY TOO HAD AN EMOTIONALLY ABUSIVE RELATIONSHIP. HE INTRODUCED HER TO THE DRUGS THAT EVENTUALLY KILLED HER. WHITNEY DIED IN 2012. THEIR DAUGHTER DIED THREE YEARS LATER, AFTER BEING FOUND UNCONSCIOUS IN THE BATHROOM OF HER APARTMENT.

'A Fool in Love' was their great success, until producer Phil Spector entered their lives with his 'Wall of Sound' production formula to record 'River Deep – Mountain High', which, while passing unnoticed in the United States, was a big hit in the United Kingdom, made them stars and resulted in them setting out on tour with The Rolling Stones in America in 1969.

Ike Turner

BEGAN USING COCAINE DURING THESE YEARS AND HIS ADDICTION SOON BECAME TOO MUCH FOR HIM, AS HE FOUND HIMSELF SPENDING MORE THAN FIFTY THOUSAND DOLLARS A MONTH. IN THE LATE SEVENTIES HE MOVED ON TO CRACK. HIS ADDICTIONS STAYED WITH HIM UNTIL HIS DEATH.

Ike and Tina achieved a series of successes, reaching their high point with *Come Together* (1970) and *Workin' Together* (1970), their first record on the

Liberty Records label, for which they recorded their greatest hit, a version of 'Proud Mary' by Creedence Clearwater Revival, which won them a Grammy for best R&B group.

> THE FIRST TIME TINA WAS PHYSICALLY ABUSED BY IKE WAS WHEN SHE TOLD HIM SHE WAS THINKING ABOUT LEAVING THE BAND. IKE HIT HER ON THE HEAD WITH A WOODEN SHOE-TREE. HE THEN FORCED HER INTO HAVING SEX. THIS MADE TINA TERRIFIED OF HIM. IN THE MIDDLE OF THE SEVENTIES SHE TOOK REFUGE IN BUDDHISM SO AS NOT TO BE DRAGGED DOWN BY HER STRESSFUL CAREER AND THE VIOLENCE METED OUT BY HER HUSBAND.

After a brutal fight in Dallas, Tina took refuge at a friend's house, and in 1976 she asked Ike for a divorce. The artist then focused on her solo career, achieving commercial success with *Private Dancer* in 1984. A few years later she had international success with *Foreign Affair* (1989). With the single 'The Best', Tina's career was unstoppable. She went on to win a total of eleven Grammy awards, three of them special honorary awards.

Ike never got over the split and he sank even further into his addictions. During the eighties he was arrested more than ten times for drug possession and went to jail twice.

In 1991, when he was in prison again, Ike and Tina Turner were inducted into the Rock & Roll Hall of Fame.

> IN 2007, IKE DIED FROM AN OVERDOSE, AND HIS AUTOPSY REVEALED THAT HE WAS TAKING SEROQUEL, A TREATMENT FOR SCHIZOPHRENIA AND BIPOLAR DISORDER.

STEVIE NICKS & LINDSEY BUCKINGHAM
(1965-1977)

The first time Stevie Nicks and Lindsey Buckingham came across one another was in secondary school in 1965. He, a year younger, was singing 'California Dreaming' by The Mamas and the Papas to some school friends, and she took it upon herself to join in with the backing vocals.

They did not see each other again until two years later, when Lindsey contacted Stevie because he needed a singer for his psychedelic rock band, Fritz. She agreed. The band began to gain popularity, and they opened for Jimi Hendrix and Janis Joplin between 1968 and 1971.

Stevie and Lindsey started a relationship when Fritz disbanded. They went on composing songs and recording demos together until the Polydor Records label released their first record, *Buckingham Nicks*, in 1973.

The album was not a great success, and they were dropped by the record label. They then began to have troubles as a couple. Their attempts at making a name for themselves were not working out, and while Lindsey toured intermittently as a guitarist with other bands, Stevie worked as a waitress and house cleaner.

Around 1974, London-based rock group Fleetwood Mac was looking for a guitarist. The band, led by drummer Mick Fleetwood, was part of the boom in British blues at the end of the sixties. In the early seventies, their formation changed several times and the band entered a critical phase.

Mick travelled to California to see producer Keith Olsen, with whom he was going to work on the band's next record at Sound City Studios. As a sample of the work of his studio, Keith played him 'Frozen Love', one of the singles from *Buckingham Nicks*. Mick, who needed a guitarist, was keen to meet Lindsey Buckingham and asked him to join Fleetwood Mac. Lindsey agreed, but only so long as Stevie Nicks was taken on as vocalist.

THE LEGENDARY

Sound City (1969-2011),

A RECORDING STUDIO IN LOS ANGELES, WORKED WITH THE LIKES OF Neil Young, Tom Petty, The Grateful Dead, Fleetwood Mac, The Black Crowes, Red Hot Chili Peppers AND Nine Inch Nails... AND PRODUCED THE LEGENDARY << Nevermind >> BY Nirvana, WHOSE DRUMMER, Dave Grohl, MADE THE DOCUMENTARY << SOUND CITY >> IN 2013, IN TRIBUTE TO THE STUDIO.

In 1975 they released *Fleetwood Mac*, with a more melodic sound, closer to soft rock. Together they went on to achieve their first number one on the Billboard 200 albums chart and sold more than five million discs.

Stevie gave them the songs she had composed a year earlier about her doubts in relation to Lindsey – 'Rhiannon' and 'Landslide' – for the album. With her voice, her styling and her compositions, she became a key component of the group and an icon of seventies rock. Margi Kent was the designer who helped her create those unique looks for the stage, with diaphanous fabrics, fringed shawls and platform boots.

On the Warner Bros. label they released *Rumours* (1977), their greatest success, which sold over twenty million copies in the US and won the Grammy Award for Album of the Year.

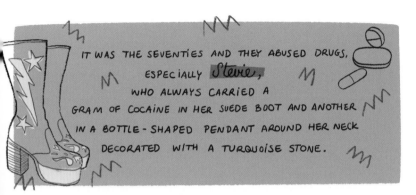

IT WAS THE SEVENTIES AND THEY ABUSED DRUGS, ESPECIALLY *Stevie*, WHO ALWAYS CARRIED A GRAM OF COCAINE IN HER SUEDE BOOT AND ANOTHER IN A BOTTLE-SHAPED PENDANT AROUND HER NECK DECORATED WITH A TURQUOISE STONE.

In spite of their success, the band was not going through the best of times on a personal level. Mick Fleetwood discovered that his wife was being unfaithful to him with his best friend. Bassist John McVie and keyboard player Christine McVie were getting a divorce. And Stevie Nicks and Lindsey Buckingham broke up after eight years together.

<< *Dreams* >>

THEIR MOST LEGENDARY SONG WAS COMPOSED BY *Stevie Nicks* AND, WITH THE REST OF THE SONGS, IS A TESTIMONIAL TO THE EMOTIONAL TURBULENCE THE BAND MEMBERS WERE GOING THROUGH.

<< *Silver Springs* >>,

WHICH WAS FINALLY FLIPPED OVER ONTO THE B-SIDE, IS DEDICATED TO HER BREAK-UP WITH *Lindsey*.

During the *Rumours* tour in November 1977, Stevie and Mick Fleetwood began a relationship, although he was still married to Jenny Boyd. It would end a short while later. Stevie's love life became unstoppable.

Jenny WAS THE SISTER OF

Pattie Boyd,

WHO WAS THE WIFE OF *George Harrison*

OF *The Beatles,*

UNTIL 1977 WHEN SHE LEFT HIM

FOR HIS BEST FRIEND,

Eric Clapton,

WHOM SHE FINALLY MARRIED IN 1979.

ERIC CLAPTON'S FAMOUS << *Layla* >>

IS DEDICATED TO PATTIE,

WHEN THEY WERE INVOLVED IN THEIR CLANDESTINE

LOVE AFFAIR.

Fleetwood Mac had already become a cult band in the eighties, and continued releasing albums throughout those years in spite of their internal troubles, much like Stevie Nicks survived her life of excesses without dying in the attempt.

On a visit to her plastic surgeon, he recommended that she stop using cocaine. She had such a big hole in her nose that she might die of a cerebral haemorrhage with the next dose. Stevie left Fleetwood Mac and went into a rehab centre.

Her battle with her addictions has been constant ever since. To overcome her anxiety and help her avoid going back to cocaine, her psychiatrist prescribed her Klonopin, which tranquillised her but left her wandering through life like a zombie, until 1995, when she stopped the therapy with the psychiatrist and went back into rehab.

The band's original formation came back together for the twentieth anniversary of the *Rumours* album, and in 1998 they entered the Rock & Roll Hall of Fame. They have been active ever since and are considered a cult band.

Lindsey Buckingham is happy with his wife and children, but he wonders what would have happened if they had not accepted Mick's offer to join the band. Stevie Nicks has never had a stable partner or any children; she has overcome her addictions and is keeping up a battle against drug use. She is considered a rock goddess by new generations of musicians, and that is her greatest gift.

NICO & JIM MORRISON (1967)

It was her beauty that took Nico to New York in 1960, although she never left Europe behind completely. A photographer in Berlin discovered this multitalented artist when she was just sixteen, and, from that moment on, her meteoric career as a model for names such as *Vogue* and Chanel took off.

IN 1959 NICO HAD TAKEN PART IN THE FILMING OF

FEDERICO FELLINI'S

<< LA DOLCE VITA >>

with

MARCELLO MASTROIANNI

In 1962 she gave birth to her only son

> ARI <

the fruit of an affair with actor Alain Delon. Delon never recognised paternity, although he and the boy were like two peas in a pod.

To begin with Nico took care of Ari in the bohemian scene of New York. The little boy became the mascot of Warhol's Factory. At the age of three, he was finishing off Bob Dylan or John Cale's cocktails and sucking amphetamines thinking they were sweets.

Seeing that she couldn't look after the child because of her lifestyle and addictions, she handed him into the care of Alain Delon's mother, who took him to Europe. When Ari came of age, he wanted to renew his relationship with his mother, but she initiated him into the use of heroin and the young man suffered an overdose, although he did eventually survive.

It was 1965 when Jim Morrison graduated from the University of California, Los Angeles, and decided to focus on what he thought was his true vocation: poetry. Jim was living in Venice Beach, on the roof of an abandoned house, and on a diet of tinned beans and LSD.

DURING THAT SUMMER OF 1965 HE WROTE THE LYRICS FOR «Moonlight Drive» & «Hello, I Love You».

Then he met Ray Manzarek, who proposed that together they form

THE DOORS

In 1966 the group got a gig at the famous Whisky a Go Go club as openers for Van Morrison's band Them. This was the first outing for the song 'The End'.

WHISKY A GO GO

OPENED IN 1964 ON SUNSET BOULEVARD
WITH GORGEOUS GO-GO DANCERS
IN 'CAGES', WHO DANCED BETWEEN
CONCERTS. IT PLAYED AN IMPORTANT
ROLE IN THE MUSICAL CAREERS OF
CALIFORNIAN ROCK BANDS SUCH AS

The Byrds Love Buffalo Springfield

Jim improvised a song that recreated the myth of Oedipus and turned 'The End' into a legend. People went into ecstasy, but it was too much for the owner of the club and he threw them out the back door. They were followed by the owner of Elektra Records, who happened to be in the audience. The group released their first album, *The Doors*, in 1967.

In 1965 Nico had had a fling with Rolling Stone

Vox Teardrop Mark VI
THE GUITAR THAT WAS CREATED FOR BRIAN JONES AND WHICH HE MADE POPULAR

Brian Jones,

who produced her first single 'I'm Not Sayin'. He took her to The Factory and introduced her to Andy Warhol, who wanted her to act in several of his experimental films, such as →

«Chelsea Girls» (1966).

THE VELVET UNDERGROUND

were hired by Warhol the same year to play live at his multimedia performance *Exploding Plastic Inevitable*, which toured the United States and Canada.

On their return, he offered to be their manager and produce their first LP, *The Velvet Underground & Nico* (1967), on which he insisted on his muse as vocalist. Among other songs, Nico sang:

<< I'll be your mirror >>

<< All Tomorrow's Parties >>   and   << Sunday Morning >>

Nico's debut solo album, *Chelsea Girl* (alluding to the film of the same name by Warhol) also came out in 1967. Bob Dylan and Jackson Browne, as well as The Velvet Underground, all collaborated on it. A short while later, Lou Reed's band dispensed with Warhol and also with Nico, who turned to focus on her solo career.

During this time Nico had a brief relationship with Lou Reed, who took inspiration from her to write the song 'I'll Be Your Mirror'. Although Nico's father died in a concentration camp during the Second World War, she is said to have been rather racist, and she soon rejected Lou on the grounds of his being Jewish.

 FINALLY FOUND HIS OTHER HALF IN

Laurie ANDERSON

A NORTH AMERICAN SINGER AND MULTIDISCIPLINARY ARTIST.
THEY FIRST MET IN THE EARLY NINETIES AND
REMAINED TOGETHER UNTIL LOU'S DEATH
IN 2013.

<< IN OUR SLEEP >>
FROM LAURIE'S ALBUM
<< *Bright Red* >>
IS A DUET WITH HER THEN FIANCÉ LOU REED.

Nico and Jim met during the 'Summer of Love'. The single 'Light My Fire', by The Doors, was number one for several weeks during those unforgettable months of 1967.

THE SUMMER OF LOVE

WAS A SOCIAL PHENOMENON THAT EMERGED IN SAN FRANCISCO IN THE SUMMER OF 1967, IN WHICH HUNDREDS OF THOUSANDS OF HIPPIES CAME TOGETHER TO CELEBRATE THE BIRTH OF A NEW COUNTERCULTURE AND TO DECLARE THEIR OPPOSITION TO THE VIETNAM WAR, CONSUMER VALUES AND RACIAL DISCRIMINATION, AS WELL AS THEIR CHAMPIONING OF COMMUNAL LIVING, THE LEGISLATION OF DRUGS AND ENVIRONMENTAL AWARENESS.

MAKE LOVE NOT WAR

End the war before it ends you.

SAY NO TO WAR

Nico and Jim were introduced at The Castle, a 1920s Los Angeles mansion rented for the band Love to live in. The members of the city's music scene would always turn up there at some point in the night. After their first meeting, Nico and Jim, tripping on LSD, began a love affair that lasted a summer. Although Jim had been going out with Pamela Courson since their university days, the couple had an open relationship, putting their own affair on hold according to their sexual impulses.

Jim and Nico liked to drive out into the desert and eat mescal. On one occasion, they cut their thumbs and intermingled their blood. Jim saw the hallucinations as acts of poetic inspiration and encouraged Nico to write her own songs while under the influence. The lyrics they composed together form part of Nico's album *The Marble Index* (1969).

NICO FELL HEAD OVER HEELS IN LOVE WITH JIM, BUT THE INTENSE ROMANCE SOON EVAPORATED AND MORRISON RETURNED TO THE ARMS OF HIS GIRLFRIEND *Pamela* COURSON

Nico's obsession with Jim led her to swap her platinum blonde for red to look more like Pamela, since he had confessed to her his weakness for redheads. She kept this hair colour until Morrison's death in the bathroom of a Paris hotel four years later.

Consumed by heroin and depression, Nico died of a brain haemorrhage after falling off a bicycle in Ibiza in 1988, when she was forty-nine.

ELIZABETH FRASER & ROBIN GUTHRIE
(1979-1998)

Robin Guthrie and his friend, bassist Will Heggie, grew up together in Grangemouth, Scotland, and in 1979 they formed Cocteau Twins, a band influenced by the likes of The Birthday Party, Siouxsie and the Banshees, and Kate Bush.

THE BAND NAME CAME FROM A SONG BY THEIR FELLOW GLASWEGIANS *Simple Minds.*

In Nash, a small local discotheque, they met Elizabeth Fraser. After a childhood marred by eating disorders and sexual abuse by her brother-in-law, she was thrown out of home at the age of sixteen because of her punk leanings. She had tattoos on her arms of her heroes, Siouxsie and the Banshees.

Siouxsie Sioux,

WHOSE REAL NAME IS SUSAN JANET BALLION,

WAS A PIONEER OF POST-PUNK ALONG WITH HER BAND

SIOUXSIE and THE BANSHEES
(1976-1996).

WITH HER HUSBAND

Budgie,

THE BAND'S DRUMMER SINCE 1979,

SHE FORMED THE PARALLEL PROJECT

The Creatures.

THE COUPLE MARRIED IN 1991

AND DIVORCED IN 2007.

THE SONG
<< *Slowdive* >>,
BY *Siouxsie and The Banshees*,
INSPIRED THE NAME OF THE BAND *Rachel Goswell*

FORMED WITH *Neil Halstead* IN 1989

WITH A SOUND SOMEWHERE BETWEEN SHOEGAZE AND DREAM POP.

THEY HAD KNOWN EACH OTHER SINCE THE AGE OF SIX

AND FIRST OF ALL WERE FRIENDS, THEN LATER LOVERS.

THEY BROKE UP SHORTLY AFTER FORMING

S L O W D I V E,

BUT EVEN SO THEY SMOOTHED THINGS OVER ENOUGH

TO CONTINUE WITH THE GROUP AND, AS IF THIS WERE

NOT ALREADY A FEAT, THEY SET UP

ANOTHER PROJECT TOGETHER IN 1994:

Mojave 3.

Robin and Elizabeth fell in love, and in 1980 Fraser joined Cocteau Twins as singer and songwriter. In 1982 they got their first recording contract with the independent label 4AD and released their album *Garlands*. Shortly afterwards, the bassist left the group and was replaced by Simon Raymond. The new formation signed a contract with Capitol Records in 1988, which gained them greater commercial visibility.

THEIR MOST WELL-KNOWN ALBUM IS
<< Heaven or Las Vegas >> (1990).

The relationship was not an easy one, but in the 90s, after the birth of their daughter, Lucy-Belle, Robin tried to leave behind his addiction to alcohol and drugs while Elizabeth started therapy to overcome her own demons.

In 1997 the trio disbanded during the recording of their ninth studio album, partly due to the irreconcilable differences between Robin and Elizabeth, who had been separated since 1993 and ended up divorcing in 1998.

ELIZABETH HAD A BRIEF AND
INTENSE ROMANCE WITH
Jeff Buckley
IN THE NINETIES.
SHE COMPLAINED TO HIM
THAT HIS CAREER WAS
EVERYTHING TO HIM.
FOR POSTERITY, LIZ AND JEFF
RECORDED THE SONG
<< *All The Flowers in Time Bend Towards The Sun* >>.
THE NEWS OF JEFF'S DEATH IN 1997
CAME WHEN SHE WAS RECORDING
<< *Teardrop* >>
WITH
Massive Attack.

WE'LL BE TOGETHER

(they are still together)

WIN BUTLER

RÉGINE CHASSAGNE

Arcade Fire

TINA WEYMOUTH

CHRIS FRANTZ

Talking Heads

PATTI SCIALFA

BRUCE SPRINGSTEEN

Bruce Springsteen and the E Street Band

SATOMI MATSUZAKI

GREG SAUNIER

Deerhoof

GEORGIA HUBLEY

IRA KAPLAN

Yo La Tengo

JAY-Z

BEYONCÉ

ALAN SPARHAWK

Low

MIMI PARKER

BRITTA PHILLIPS

DEAN WAREHAM

Luna

135

TRACEY THORN

BEN WATT

Everything But The Girl

ADAM HOROVITZ

KATHLEEN HANNA

ELVIS COSTELLO

DIANA KRALL

VÍCTOR MANUEL

ANA BELÉN

GLORIA ESTEFAN

EMILIO ESTEFAN

ALICIA KEYS

SWIZZ BEATZ

\\\ | | | //

(and the odd few more)

touch wood.

// | \ \

<< You know my love goes with you,
as your love stays with me.>>

Leonard Cohen

For D.A., my love (for now).